Miraculous

WALTER ROUZER

MIRACULOUS

Peak Wave Publishing

peakwave.org

ISBN 978-0-9970304-0-2

Author contact: http://www. wrouzer.com

TO WALLY, PAM, JESSICA,
KIMBERLY AND IRIS

CHAPTER 1

I always tried to believe in miracles. I always hoped and prayed for one. Something happened that would change my life forever.

I'm Hailee Tupper, and this is my life story.

I'll always remember the message I received from my guardian angel, "When your pain becomes so great you think you cannot bear it, you will have unspeakable joy, if you endure the trials, keep the faith, and live a life in love and kindness for others."

November 17, 1871, Bristol Bay, England

Brunsville Zoo keeper, Joseph Higgins, stared at me through the iron bars of my exhibit. I was not an animal or something to be feared and put on public display, even if I didn't look human, but that was my place. Higgins told me the story of my beginning. He said he remembered the details all too well.

It was a dark stormy night when he lit the oil lamps and shouted out across the zoo grounds for Miss Finch, the head veterinarian, to hurry up and get inside the carriage. He squinted through heavy sheets of rain, trying to keep his horses centered on a narrow road, bordered by hundred foot cliffs. The wind blew in great gusts, rocking the carriage side to side, nearly tipping it over.

He said on that night in particular, Miss Finch looked like death warmed over. Her black hooded coat cloaked her white, half-mooned cheeks deep in shadow as she stared straight ahead with large, doll like eyes.

He felt the sting of cold blow against his face as he pressed the horses onward for about an hour longer before reaching my parents' house, a mud brick building with a straw thatched roof, located by the edge of the forest. Higgins took a deep breath and smelled the scent of pine blended with the pungent fragrance of sage.

The carriage came to a sudden stop in front of my parents' house at exactly midnight. The numbing cold nearly froze his hands around the reins. A howling wind swept the trees from side to side, and one could hear the tips of their branches screech against the windowpanes, as if pleading to come inside to escape the storm's thrashing.

They stepped down from the carriage, then hurried past the white picket fence, and across the brown cobblestone pathway leading to the front of the house. Higgins reached out and was about to knock on the front door, when it suddenly opened before him. My dad, Devin Tupper, a tall, thin man, with a squared-off chin, pleaded with them to hurry inside, saying his wife, my mom Clarabelle, was about to give birth.

Higgins said the first thing that caught his attention upon entering the house were baskets of mushrooms. They were everywhere. He said my mom was crazy about eating mushrooms, all different kinds, colors, and shades, even exotic ones, and ones that probably should never have been eaten. There were baskets of them by the front entrance, living room, kitchen, and even by the bedside where my mom waited impatiently to have her baby... waited to have me.

The storm raged on as everyone nervously awaited my birth. Deep rumblings and explosive bursts of lightning flickered light through the windows. Rain beat upon the rooftop, and one could hear the constant dripping of water through the thatched ceiling into a wooden bucket at the far corner of the room.

Miss Finch stepped into the bedroom wearing her black hooded coat, wrinkled black pants, and thick leather boots.

Mom quickly leaned up in bed, rubbing and blinking her eyes. "Who's that?" she asked.

My dad walked up to her bedside, clasped her small hands, and smiled. "She's the doctor who's going to help deliver our baby."

Mom shook her head. "Doctor? Did you say doctor?" She pointed at Miss Finch. "But she doesn't look like a doctor."

"Doc Reeder got an emergency call," said dad. "He's on the other side of town treating rancher Billings, who got gored by one of his bulls."

Dad watched Miss Finch place a steaming hot bowl of water on the dresser beside the bed, then remove several white clothes from her brown leather bag.

"She's the only other doctor available this time of night," he said, smiling at mom. "I was told that she has plenty of experience delivering babies, even though she's only a zoo veterinarian."

When Mom heard that, her mouth dropped open. "Veterinarian! Veterinarian!" She took two deep breaths. "You fetched a veterinarian to help deliver our baby?"

"Now, now," said Miss Finch, stepping forward. "Nothing to get upset about." She reached down and placed her reassuring hand on her shoulder. "I successfully delivered many babies in the past, but I have to confess that this will be the first time I'll be assisting to deliver a baby without a tail."

"Did you say without a tail!"

"Tails or no tails," said Miss Finch with a grin. "You can trust me to deliver your baby."

Mom raised her hand up against her forehead, looking as if she was about to faint, then reached out for a half-full bowl full of mushrooms on the dresser counter. Dad rushed over and snatched the bowl away before she could lay her hand on a single one. "You couldn't possibly be thinking about eating another mushroom now," said dad. "Remember what Doc Reeder said?"

Mom gave a heavy sigh. "Oh… you worry about too many things. They're just healthy food." She reached out for the bowl. "Give me just one more. What harm could just one more mushroom do? I need one to help calm me down."

CHAPTER 2

At half past midnight, out from the womb I came. Miss Finch whisked me up into her arms and carried me to the far side of the room, all the while keeping her back to my mother.

"Well, what's wrong?" said Mom, leaning up in bed. "Let me see my baby!"

Miss Finch looked back over her shoulder, forced a smile, and announced, "It's a girl!"

"Let me see my baby!" Mom stretched her arms toward me. "Bring her to me!"

Miss Finch slowly stepped toward her bed, but then suddenly stopped halfway across the room.

Mom's eyes widened, and her breathing deepened. "Bring my daughter to me now! Are you deaf? Didn't you hear me? I want to see my baby!"

With a solemn look on her face, Miss Finch

walked up to her bedside.

Mom's eyes narrowed. "Well, come on. Hand her to me!"

The instant mom saw me she screamed so loud, Higgins said she could be heard nearly a mile away. It was a scream of disbelief, and of horror. Higgins said her voice must have scared me mute, because right after she screamed I looked like I wanted to cry, but nothing came out. My mouth repeatedly opened and closed, over and over again, but nothing came out. Not even a peep.

Was it the shock of my mom's scream right after birth that made me mute, or was it a physical ailment? No one could figure it out for sure, not even the doctor. Higgins said I came out looking like some kind of mushroom monster with a grey moldy looking face and body.

Mom turned her head away from me and said, "She doesn't even look human. I can't even bear to look at her."

The floorboards bowed and creaked beneath Miss Finch's black leather boots as she stepped up to my dad with me cradled in her arms. She offered to take care of me, and raise me as her own. She even promised my parents that they could come visit me anytime.

Dad shook his head. "How could we give

up our only daughter, even if she doesn't look human?"

Miss Finch showed my face to my dad again. He reached out to touch my grey moldy face, but quickly pulled his hand back. He stepped away from me, then raised his hand up against his forehead, looking as if he suddenly turned ill. Higgins said he saw beads of sweat roll down my dad's forehead and drip onto the floor.

After my parents shed many a tear, they finally agreed to let Miss Finch give me a good home.

"I think you made the right decision," said Miss Finch. "You won't have any regrets. You have my word on taking good care of the child."

Higgins walked up to me and stared deep into my eyes, the window of my soul. "I can see something special, dear, and beautiful coming from within, beneath the outer layer of her moldy looking skin."

"Higgins," said Miss Finch, "I think you imagine too many things."

Right as Miss Finch was about to leave, she looked back over her shoulder at my parents and said, "What name did you choose for the child?"

My dad spoke up. "We already decided, that if it was a girl, her name would be Hailee."

Miss Finch grinned and smiled down at me.

"Very well then, Hailee it is. Hailee Tupper."

******

Higgins said he couldn't understand why Miss Finch's sad look all of a sudden turned into a big smile the instant she stepped into the carriage. As a matter of fact, he said her smile stayed with her all the way back to the zoo.

******

When they arrived at the zoo, Miss Finch stepped down from the carriage, rocked me in her arms and gave me a big grin. "This creature," she said, referring to me, "is going to bring the zoo a lot of extra money and get me a big raise so I can afford a larger house. I might even be able to retire early."

Higgins shook his head. "But you be promising her parents that you would be givin' her a good, proper home. Don't be so greedy."

Miss Finch chuckled. "Greed? Who's greedy?" She reached into her side pocket and pulled out a piece of chocolate. "Have one?"

"No, and stop tryin' to be always be gettin' your way with a little bit of chocolate."

"Well... she's not going to fit in anywhere else," she argued. "If not here, then where? Come now, should we arrange to put this little monster in some kind of traveling circus like I had to suffer as an orphan child with no family and stable home? Get your senses, Higgins." She aimed her finger at him. "You'll see that the logical place for her is right here at the zoo." She put on a sweet smile. "Don't you know that kids everywhere love animals?" She swiped her hand at Higgins and chuckled. "Come on, it could be a real life animal paradise for her staying here." She smiled down at me and tickled my chin. "You're a lucky little baby monster, aren't you?" She turned toward Higgins and said, "She'll be in a nice large enclosure, next to an exhibit that has a cute tiger on one side, and on the other side, a big lovable gorilla." She gave him a lopsided smile. "Everyone knows kids love tigers and monkeys."

Higgins stepped up to Miss Finch and tried to pry me out of her arms. "Give her to me! Give her to me now!"

Miss Finch stepped back and shook her head.

Higgins glared into her eyes. "I won't let you be doing this horrible thing!" He stepped closer. "It's not right to be exhibiting her in a zoo, like an animal!" He reached out a second time and tried to take me out of her arms. "Give her to me! Give her to me now! The zoo is no place to raise a child! Besides, the caves here are cold and damp, with the smell of animal waste."

Miss Finch suddenly jumped two feet back, seeing a large cockroach scurry across the ground in front of her. "Dirty, filthy bugs! Disgusting creatures!" she shouted, taking several more steps back.

Higgins chuckled. "Why you be such afraid of a little bug?"

"Only cockroaches. I sprayed a bunch of them in my house last week. Before the dreadful little creatures had the chance to die they tried to attack me by flying on my face and neck while I laid in bed. The filthy, dirty bugs had a leader too. He was the giant of the lot. Biggest, ugliest bug I ever laid my eyes on. I called him Daddy Goose Bump, because he was so horrible looking, the hairs on my arm stood straight up."

"Cockroaches don't be havin' names, get revenge, or be having a leader." Higgins chuckled. "Perhaps you just be havin' a creepy nightmare. What be happening if word got out that you be terrified of such little bugs, or that you be giving names to such?"

Miss Finch reached out and pushed Higgins back. "You better keep quiet about this, or I'll... I'll have you fired!"

"Maybe Daddy Goose Bump will be gettin' you first."

"No, I'm sure the bug spray got him. Just haven't found him yet. I'm sure he's curled up somewhere in my house."

Higgins squinted and pointed at her. "You be a heartless woman."

She raised her chin at Higgins. "If I was heartless, I wouldn't have offered to give this little monster a stable home."

"You mean cave home."

"Oh... what's the difference? It's still stable, isn't it? More than I had growing up." She smiled down at me, and then rocked me in her arms. "I just want to protect her." She stepped up to Higgins and poked his chest with her finger. "What better way of protecting her than by putting her in a secure place where people can't hurt her?"

Higgins reached out for me. "A cold cave be no home for anyone, besides, she needs a "real" mother and dad, and to be treated with kindness and love!"

Miss Finch gave him a sharp slap on the side of the shoulder. "Come on, who would be willing to do that for this little monster?"

Higgins pointed at himself. "I would."

Miss finch tilted her head to one side and

locked eyes with him. "Yes... I suppose you would care enough for this little monster to give her the attention she needs."

Higgins nodded. "I be insisting to help her, every way I can."

She pointed her finger at him. "Not during your work hours!"

"OK, then I be doing it during the evening time. I be not a professional teacher, but I be doing the best job I can to help her to learn."

And so it came to pass, I was raised and cared for like a tiger cub, without its mother, with a bottle, in a crib, in a dark cave, in between two other wild animal exhibits.

CHAPTER 3

Miss Finch had me work for food from the time I was an infant. Even when I was still a baby and couldn't yet walk, she would take my crib out of the cave home and display me before the zoo visitors. When I grew old enough to walk, the only life I knew was in the zoo. I was forced to go outside and just stand on the grassy area so people could stare at me.

"You're a darling little monster," she said, patting me on the head. "It won't be so bad here. I had to work hard as an orphan child just to survive in this world, and you can too."

During the first years of my life I was so terrified of being put on display, I would try to hide behind the boulders, trees, and bushes in my exhibit.

Miss Finch would always find me, sway her head side to side and say, "So this is where you're hiding today." She would pull me out from my hiding place by the arm and drag me back to the middle of the grass area, then smile at the zoo visitors and say, "Sorry, this won't happen again. Everyone will have a chance to see the Mushroom Monster. She's just a tad shy today, that's all."

After the zoo closed Miss Finch would come up to me, grab me by my arm, and say, "Remember, you little monster, the bigger the crowd, the more money you bring to the zoo, and the more food you'll get for supper."

She sneered down at me with her thick, low set eyebrows, that reminded me of a bird of prey, like a hawk or eagle.

"And if you should happen to disappoint the crowd, like today," said Miss Finch, with a scowl on her face, "you'll get nothing to eat. Remember that."

Sometimes I thought deep inside that I was like regular people, and dreamed that my face, arms and legs, looked just like the zoo visitors, so I would be free to leave this horrible life. I thought about running away, and even sailing across the ocean to a land where people actually love and care for one another.

At the end of each day, right after the zoo closed, I would drag my feet back into my cave and stand before my only possession, a cracked mirror Miss Finch hung on the cave wall to remind me that I was not like them. I looked at my hands and could see signs that I was like them... the humans. I knew one thing for sure in my heart: I'm not some kind of beast to be laughed and mocked at. I would often stare at my reflection in the mirror and ask myself, *what am I?*

As I stood before the zoo guests, I would often take note of their beautiful clothes and shiny hair. I often dreamed of having clean, shiny hair, and spotless warm clothes, like those staring back at me from the other side of the fence. Then, a moment later, I would blink my eyes and be brought back into reality, hearing cruel words shouted at me, and see rotten vegetables fly over the fence and splatter against my body.

******

The food that I was served at the zoo wasn't fit for a pig. Thank goodness for Higgins. He was kind enough to sneak special foods and snacks to me. I knew he didn't make much money working at the zoo, and felt so thankful for his giving nature.

Higgins was nearly bald, and had a "melon-shaped" head. Deep creases ran across his forehead. Even though he had only a little bit of hair on top of his head, I would often see him comb it to keep what was left looking neat. What I liked most about the way he looked were his large kindly eyes, bushy eyebrows, and the way he always seemed to carry the warmth of a smile wherever he went.

One day, at a very early age, when I first began to understand words, Higgins reached through the iron bars, placed his hand upon my shoulder, and told me my given name... "Hailee Tupper."

With tears swelling in his eyes, he also told me the meaning of the words on the sign that hung above the cave, the zoo exhibit that Miss Finch destined to be my home. It said, "The Mushroom Monster." He said that's what people thought I looked like.

One morning, Miss Finch gave me some ugly clothes to wear. "Here's a short-sleeved black shirt and pants to put on," she snarled. "I want people to see your arms and legs so they can mock at your ugliness."

I cried many nights by myself in that cold damp cave. The only true friend I ever had was Higgins. He always tried to teach me new things.

One night he came to me and said, "Hailee, always be remembering, every human, animal, and even the insects are precious, having a special purpose in life."

Higgins kindhearted way of thinking about life must have deeply affected me, because even when I saw such a lowly creature as a worm after a heavy rain struggling upon the ground, I would pick it up in the palm of my hand, dig a little hole, and gently cover it with dirt. I thought Higgins was right when he said that all life is precious. I felt warm inside knowing that even such a lowly creature as a worm now had a second chance at life. Everything deserves a good life. Everything deserves to live.

******

One evening, Higgins sat in front of me and told me about his childhood. "Hailee," he said, "I experienced many hardships in life, just like you. Raised in a small, three bedroom house I was. It leaned to one side, and I be always worried that it might collapse on me or family at any time. During the evenings, my mom, dad, three brothers, and five sisters would be offering prayers of thanks to God for the large pot placed at the center of our dinner table. Most evenings it be filled with just hot water, cabbage and a couple potatoes." Higgins suddenly gripped his arm, looking as if he was in a little bit of pain. "Darn shoulder, always be givin' me trouble. Too much heavy lifting as a child. Where did I leave off? Oh yes... when I be still quite a young lad, I needed to help put food on the family table by working at Montgomery Textiles, located on the other side of town." He raised his hand in front of me. "See this scar on my thumb?"

I nodded.

"I be gettin' that from working at the mill." He shook his head. "Mr. Peabody, the owner, should never be letting children work there. One day I be telling him straight on, not to be letting children work at his factory. Got fired, I did, for standing up to that greedy Mr. Peabody. I be very thankful to later get hired here at the zoo, because I love to be takin' care of animals. My bother Elroy, helps me to be takin' care of the zoo grounds a couple days a week. He loves all different kinds of animals, just like me. If anything should be happening to me, Elroy would likely be takin' my place. He be a good man."

He held a book up in front of me. "My parents couldn't afford to send me, nor my brothers and sisters to be gettin' a formal education. Mom, every evening, bless her soul, tried to teach us how to read the best she could."

Higgins's serious look suddenly blossomed into a big smile. "Hailee, despite the hard life growing up, the most important thing about family life be that I was raised in a "God-fearing" home filled with love. I be so blessed and thankful that my parents taught me the importance of love, forgiveness, and compassion for all living creatures.

Music also be an important part of my life. My parents taught me, and my brothers and sisters, how to be singin' many beautiful, spiritual songs."

I loved to hear Higgins sing. He sang precious songs of joy, beauty, and of redemption. He was blessed with such a wonderful singing voice. "Amazing Grace" was my favorite song he taught me. I listened carefully to all the words and notes to his songs, memorizing them all by heart. As he sang to me, I often wished and wondered how lovely it would be if I wasn't mute, and had a voice to sing along with him.

Higgins had another gift from God, and that was being an artist, although he didn't start out that way. He was able to teach me all about the outside world and what it looked like through his drawings and paintings. He began by just doing simple line sketches with a pencil. As the days, months, and years passed by, his drawings began to look more lifelike. I was delighted when he started working with colored paints. I would never have known what beautiful colors existed in nature outside my cage if it weren't for his paintings.

Higgins eventually made hundreds of drawings and paintings for me to look at. There were scenes of people, pets, wildlife, towns, and just about everything else. His early works of art weren't that good, but as he kept on practicing, over time, he became a master at creating beautiful paintings.

Higgins smiled. "Hailee, I be never acquiring such a skill for drawing and painting if it not be for my love in showing you what the outside world be looking like."

By pointing at objects, people and places in his art, and then showing me written words to go along with them, he was able to teach me the meaning of a great many words. I wished that I looked normal and was free to travel and see in real life all the beautiful images in his paintings.

Although I was mute, and couldn't tell him directly, I hoped that he would someday have the chance to show his paintings before important people and make a good living selling them.

I would often see him with droopy eyes, sitting slouched forward, elbows resting on his knees, looking so exhausted after a long day at work. In spite of feeling so tired, he still managed to spend a couple hours each night to teach me all about the outside world, in all its splendor, and all its dangers.

Higgins also taught me what he knew about history and geography, and even brought me a map, from which I learned all about my city and country.

******

I would often sit in my cold, damp cave, beside my lantern, and think; everyone deserves to have a better life than this, even if they thought of me as some kind of monster.

I cared for and loved everything that God created. I wished and prayed for just one word of kindness, from one zoo visitor, but I never heard a single one.

I felt so sad that I never had the chance to get to know my parents. I sat on my bed, with my hands folded together, and prayed each night that they would come deliver me from this nightmare of a life. I dreamed about what my mother and father might look like, and what they might be doing.

I would stare toward the back end of my cave, trying to convince myself that this would be the day they would come to my rescue, and set me free. But sadly, they never came.

I wished and prayed that I had a mother and father who would wrap their arms around me in love, just like the families I would see every day walking up and down the zoo pathway. I wished I had a pretty dress, instead of rags. I wished I had a soft bed, instead of my hard wooden bench with its bumpy splinters. It was hard as a rock, and oft times felt as cold as the ground beneath my shoes, each having two holes worn clear through.

Though I couldn't speak, I was able through making gestures with my hands and face let Higgins know that I wanted to be with my mother and father. He came to me one night and said, "Hailee, I be goin' up to the mountain today, to the place you be born, and try find your parents."

But when he came back later in the day, he said that they were nowhere to be found. My heart sank low when I heard that. I felt so alone.

"Hailee," said Higgins, "I even traveled to

neighboring villages, knocked door to door, I did, but still be unable to be findin' your parents."

Miss Finch would always get tight-lipped whenever Higgins brought up the subject of where my parents might have moved to. I suppose, with all the money she was making off me at the zoo, any thought of trying to locate my parents would be the furthest thing from her mind. I took a deep breath, with my head and shoulders slumped low, and thought that they must be dead, or didn't know about my life here. No parent, I believe, would be willing to suffer their child to such a life as mine, even if I wasn't considered to be human.

CHAPTER 4

Before I was brought to the zoo as a baby, many changes were made to the exhibits to make them look more like that found in nature, including open grass areas and plant life. A wide moat, about eight feet deep, was kept filled with water at the front of the each exhibit to keep the animals from trying to escape. I didn't know how to swim, so trying to escape that way would be difficult and dangerous.

The zoo had three cave exhibits. There was one each for the tiger, gorilla, and myself. Mine was in between the other two animal exhibits. The caves were made of cement, colored and textured to look like grayish stone. Each cave was about thirty feet long, twelve feet wide, and nine feet high. At the back end of the caves were iron bars, with a padlocked door that faced the service

25

road. The opposite end of the cave opened up to a large grass area that faced the moat and fence, through which the zoo visitors could watch the animals and me.

Toward the back end of my cave, on one side, I could look through the side bars and see a silver-back gorilla they called Igor. Actually, he had very little silver fur on his back. He looked kind of funny because most of his silver fur was from the waist down, making him look like he was wearing silver pants. He liked to play a game with me to see who could do the best job at beating your chest, or scratch under the armpits. I think he always won the chest beating contest, while I did a better job at scratching under my arms. If Igor thought he won, he would beat his chest, make three grunts, then raise his arms high above his head as his way of telling me that he was the champion.

Once I bravely, or perhaps foolishly, placed my hand through the bars of his cage. Igor reached out with his massive hand and we touched fingertips. I thought that was really neat. It was like we became sort of monster friends.

On the opposite side of my cave, toward the back, gazing through the side bars, I could see a beautiful tiger. Higgins said that she was going to have cubs soon. She was almost as popular as my exhibit, and actually liked to lounge around on the outside grass area where the visitors could watch her. She had a better life than I did, because no one ever shouted cruel words at her, or threw rotten food over the fence.

******

One evening, as Higgins sat in front of me, he said, "Hailee... I truly be believin' with all my heart, that someday you will be havin' a victory over all the trials in your life." He raised his hand, closed his palm into a fist, then pointed his index and middle finger straight up, forming the letter "V".

"Hailee," he said, "do you know what this "V" letter be standin' for?"

I shook my head.

"The "V" be standin' for victory. Keep the faith and some day you will have victory in life, no matter what be standin' in your way."

I raised my hand and copied the sign of victory.

"Yes, that be it, Hailee," he said, watching me make a perfect "V" with my fingers.

"From now on, whenever we see each other,

let's be givin' the victory sign. We "will" succeed!"

Higgins smiled and pointed toward the gorilla exhibit. When I turned to see what it was, I smiled and chuckled, seeing Igor staring back at us in his cage with his hand raised high, giving us the victory sign with his two giant fingers. I thought it was pretty amazing that he was able to figure out how to copy us that quickly.

"See that," said Higgins. "Even Igor believes that you'll be havin' ah victory."

CHAPTER 5

Hailee, come see!" Higgins shouted excitedly. "The mom tiger had two boy cubs."

I was so happy when I heard that, I ran as fast as I could to the back of my cave and peered through the side bars. My eyes stretched wide seeing the mom laying on her side with her two cubs feeding on her milk. They were so lucky to have a caring, loving mother to look after them. I even felt a little jealous.

******

One day, after the tiger cubs grew old enough to eat solid food, I heard Miss Finch talking to someone by the back service road. I was curious as to what she was up to, so I walked along the side of the cave, so as not to be seen. I peeked around the edge of the wall and saw Miss Finch chatting with a man she called Sir Gumtree. He had a black pointed mustache and was dressed in tan shorts, a white striped shirt, knee-high socks, and had on a broad-rimmed, brown leather hat.

"When do you want the mom and one of the cubs?" asked Miss Finch.

Sir Gumtree gave her a serious look. "I need to take delivery tomorrow. I have an important client requesting a tiger hunt at the reserve. He's paying a nice sum to add such a beast to his mantle collection. As for the cub, he'll be ready for a hunt in a few month's time."

When I heard that, my hands curled into a tight fist, and my face flushed red. I thought, *I can't let this happen!* I looked around me, but what could I do? How could I stop it? I remembered seeing Miss Finch hide a second set of keys under a wooden crate on the other side of the road by the storage shed. I thought, *if I could just figure out some way to get my hands on those keys, then maybe I could escape at night and take the tigers with me.*

I just couldn't let Miss Finch sell the mother and one of her cubs to be hunted for sport. I stepped in plain view of Miss Finch, stuck my hands out through the bars, and shook my fists at the both of them.

"Excuse me one moment, Sir Gumtree," said Miss Finch. "I have a brief matter to attend to." She stomped up to me, then pointed at my face. "See here, you little snoop! Well... so you heard our private business affair, did you?"

I nodded, then reached through the bars and tried to grab her jacket, but she took a step back before I could get hold of it. She turned toward the man and smiled. "I'll be right with you, Sir Gumtree."

She placed her hands firmly on her hips and gave me a mean look. "How dare you try and lay a hand on me, you little monster!" She raised her chin, chuckled, then sneered at me. "Well, if you could only talk, then maybe you might be able warn someone, wouldn't you?" She leaned forward, stuck her face close to mine, and whispered into my ear, "Would you like a nice "warm" tiger rug for your cave?"

I was so mad when I heard her say that.

******

When Higgins came by later that evening, he said, "Hailee, what's wrong? I've never be seein' your face look so flushed before."

I used a stick to scratch a picture in the dirt of

Miss Finch and Sir Gumtree holding a gun pointed at a tiger. Then I drew a line out from the gun toward the tiger. Next, I drew a picture of a tiger laying on its side, like it was shot.

Higgins scratched his head and gave me a confused look. "Hailee, I be not sure what you be tryin' to tell me."

******

Early the next morning I heard some loud voices by the service road. I rushed to the back of the cave and saw Higgins arguing with Miss Finch and Sir Gumtree. That same moment, two workers I've never seen before were trying to get the mom tiger and one of the cubs into the back of a large truck.

Higgins pointed at the tigers. "Where be those men taking the mom and cub?"

Miss Finch stepped up to Higgins and stared him straight in the eye. "If you must know, my business friend here, Sir Gumtree, is taking the tigers to a game reserve where they will have lots of food to eat, and a big area to roam around in, just like they were free."

Sir Gumtree grinned. "True indeed, this zoo can't be compared to the size of land I offer them to freely roam about."

Higgins's face flushed red. "You wouldn't be takin' them to a game reserve to be hunted down for sport, would you?"

Sir Gumtree and Miss Finch exchanged glances in silence.

"Do you think I would do that?" said Miss Finch.

Higgins nodded.

"Well, they're going, and that's that!"

Higgins stomped up to the back of the truck and tried to force the back door open to let the tigers out, but the two men grabbed his arms from behind and held him back. Higgins shook himself free and chased after the truck a short ways before he ran out of breath. He looked back down the road at Miss Finch with narrowed eyes, and shouted, "You can't be getin' away with this! I be tellin' Mr. Brunsky, I will!"

Miss Finch chuckled. "Go ahead. He was the one who sealed the deal, and for quite a nice sum, I might say."

Higgins dragged his feet over to my cage with his head hung low. "Sorry Hailee, there be nothing more I could do about it. You heard Miss Finch be telling me the tiger and cub would be goin' to a reserve with lots of food, and a big place for them to be roaming around. We got no proof for the hunting."

I clenched the iron bars with my fists in frustration, feeling so helpless for not being able to prevent the tigers from being taken away.

******

I named the cub that was left behind Zebu, from one of the stories Higgins told me about a family of tigers.

Zebu turned out to be nothing like his mom and acted very shy, even though he was a boy tiger. He refused to go out of the cave so all the people could stare at him.

Early in the morning I heard Miss Finch shout at the tiger cub, "You little coward! Get out there this minute so the visitors can see you." She walked up to him and repeatedly kicked straw up into his face. "No food for you come evening. How many days of going hungry will it take before you learn to obey me?"

The following morning I was awakened by a sharp noise coming from inside the tiger's cage. When I ran over to see what it was, I saw Miss Finch snapping a leather whip close to Zebu. He backed away, then growled and pawed the air at her.

I was so mad when I saw her do that, I picked up some dirt clods and threw them through the iron bars at her.

Miss Finch squinted at me with a wrinkled nose. "You little monster!" she shouted. "How dare you throw dirt at me!" She turned and snapped the end of the whip through my cage bars. Before she had the chance to pull it back I was able to grab hold of the end of the whip, and started a tug of war with her. I caught her off balance, and was able for a moment pull the whip out of her hands, and partially back into my cage, but then tripped backwards and lost control of it.

"Why you little monster!" she shouted. "Any more trouble out of you and you'll get no food for supper, just like the tiger."

******

Zebu became very skinny, weak, and sickly, because he wouldn't listen to her and get enough food. No matter how much Miss Finch punished him, he still refused to go out of the cave and entertain the guests like the other animals.

Day after day, Miss Finch entered the tiger cage, snapped the whip near Zebu, then kicked straw up into his face to try to scare him out.

I could tell that Zebu was developing a deeper, growing hatred toward Miss Finch. I could see it in the expression on his face and in his eyes. I wouldn't want to think what might happen to her someday, when Zebu got a little bigger, if he ever caught her without her whip.

Igor jumped up and down and beat his chest whenever he heard Miss Finch snap the whip. I bet when Igor heard that, and Zebu growling back, he thought that the tiger cub was in some kind of trouble and wanted to help him fight back.

It became painful for me to stare through the bars and see Zebu getting so thin. I made a vow to myself that someday I would find a way to escape from this prison, and when I did, I would find a way back here and free Zebu.

I shared as much of my food as I could each day with Zebu to help him get stronger. He had a big appetite, so I could only give him so much food, or I would end up starving myself. Higgins tried to sneak extra meat to the cub whenever he could as well.

CHAPTER 6

"Get out, monster! Get out! We want to see the monster! Where's the monster?" The shouts from the zoo visitors' were my alarm clock to wake up and get out of the cave.

Early in the morning Miss Finch would often stand by the back service road, rub her hands together, and say, "You little creature. Do I have to come here every single morning to get you up?" Then she would point her finger at me and say, "Get out, and stand in front of those paying customers! Too bad you're mute. If you could only growl at the people, then you might be worth even more money to me and the zoo. And don't get too close to the water. I wouldn't want to lose a feature attraction like you because you drowned trying to cross the moat."

Even though I didn't know how to swim, I was

still determined to try and find a way to escape from my exhibit.

After the zoo closed one evening, I tried to make a bridge to cross the mote by breaking off several branches from the trees, then tie them together with vines. I was able to get to the other side of the moat and climb over the fence, but only got a short distance away from the zoo before they spotted me, and brought me back. They trimmed off all the lower tree branches so I couldn't try to escape that way again.

******

I saw a young boy with red hair and freckles reach into a paper bag, then pull out a large rotten tomato.

I shook my head, knowing what he had in mind to do with it, and it wasn't to give to his mother to put in his sandwich. I thought, *that's it, I can't take this anymore!* The boy arched his arm back, squinted at me, then heaved the tomato over the fence. I was somehow able to reach up and catch it in my palms without having it splatter all over myself. The little kid looked surprised that I was able to catch it. I squinted dead ahead, with the tomato arched back over my shoulder, ready to throw it right back, but the little coward darted behind his mother for protection. I thought, *at least his head is showing. This is my chance to teach that little brat some manners.*

I took careful aim, and was about to heave the tomato back at him, when I heard Miss Finch's voice echo through the opposite end of the cave. "You little monster! Don't even think about throwing that tomato! What you're holding is all you're getting for supper tonight!"

I held the tomato up to my nose and smelled it. It was rotten to the core, just like that little kid. I let it fall to the ground and went without having any food that night. Although my stomach grumbled from hunger, it was nothing compared to the hurt I felt in my spirit from having to listen to the zoo visitors' cruel words.

I often thought that it was a good thing that I was mute, because if I had my tongue, I don't know what might come out of my mouth. I might be tempted to tell those kids off, and Miss Finch too, for that matter.

I thought that Miss Finch, the kids, parents, everyone, were addicted to screaming and yelling at me. I wondered how one human could treat another person like that.

I thought that the zoo visitors probably didn't

really hate me. Perhaps they just thought of me as entertainment, someone to mock at, or to make them feel bigger than they really are. People can be so cruel at times.

I walked to the back of my cave, then gazed through the bars and out across the countryside. I thought, *there must be more good people like Higgins out there.* I just wished they would come to the zoo so they could help teach others not to be so cruel, and show a little kindness toward me. Couldn't the parents teach their kids anything about the importance of being kind to others? Didn't they learn anything at school about showing love and compassion to those who were less fortunate than themselves?

CHAPTER 7

Higgins sat outside my cell one evening and started to paint pictures of angels. "Hailee," he said, "it be important to have faith, and be believin' in the things that can't be seen. In the depths of the deepest darkness, a shining light of hope exists for all to take hold of through faith." He gazed up into the night sky. "I often be makin' special prayers that you be delivered from all this. I be believin' that a miracle can and will happen to you someday." He turned and looked me straight in the eye. "Miracles do happen, and I be believin' one will change your life forever."

******

I was able to keep the light of faith in my heart beating through the dark, dreary days and years as they slowly crept by, that is, until now. I felt so depressed I didn't think I could survive one more day of pain and torment, being treated so cruelly by the zoo visitors.

Ten o'clock that evening, I walked outside my cave and gazed up toward the stars. It was very peaceful that night, and I so much enjoyed the quiet peacefulness. It made me feel closer to God. I loved the sounds of nature, like the crickets chirping, frogs croaking, and even hearing my friend Igor snoring in the cave next door.

Like many nights before, I made a special prayer to be delivered from this body and place. I finally reached the breaking point, and came to believe that all was lost. Facing the moat, I took three steps toward the pool of water. As if in a trance, I took five more steps toward the moat. Moments later, I found myself standing by the moat's edge, staring down at my reflection on the water's surface. *It looked so peaceful and calm down there... so inviting. Why couldn't life be as such?* There was a full moon out that night, and I was able to see all the way down to the cement bottom of the pool. I inched closer and felt my body leaning over the edge.

It was during this final day and moment of despair, when I was about to give up, that something miraculous happened. Amongst the multitude of heavenly lights, I caught sight of a shooting star. I had witnessed many a shooting star in the past, but this one appeared to be very special and odd. It looked as if it was heading straight toward earth, as a matter of fact, heading straight where I was standing. The sky quickly grew brighter and brighter until it was almost blinding. I raced across the grass to the safety of the cave. A moment later, I was startled to see a glowing sphere of light flash down in front of the cave opening. It hovered about three feet off the ground several seconds, then started to float inside. I backed away from the light until I felt the heels of my shoes brush up against the cave wall. The ball of light quickly grew in size. My lips parted, and eyes stretched wide, seeing an angel step out from the light. She looked just like one of the angels in Higgins's paintings. *But how could he know what a real angel looked like?*

She had shining hair and the most beautiful smile. Her skin was so bright it almost appeared to glow. She spoke to me in soft, whispery words that seemed to float upon the air. "I heard your prayer," she said, "and I know your sorrow. Listen carefully, my child. When your pain becomes so great you think you cannot bear it, you will have unspeakable joy, if you endure the trials, keep the faith, and live a life in love and kindness for others."

I wished at that moment that I could speak. I had so many things I wished to ask her, but being mute, I couldn't get even say a single word. I wondered how I could have joy when I was trapped in this monstrous body, held captive in a prison zoo, and treated worse than an animal. Gazing into her eyes, I somehow felt that she could understand my every thought.

She spoke to me again. "Bear the pain and trials, and you will have unspeakable joy." She repeated that message to me over and over again, each time her voice growing softer, until moments later, she vanished into the sphere of light from whence she came.

The ball of light floated out of the cave, then flashed back up into the heavens.

I thought, what did she mean when she said, "When your pain becomes so great you think you cannot bear it, you will have unspeakable joy, if you endure the trials, keep the faith, and live a life in love, and kindness for others?"

I gazed toward the back of the cave and saw Igor and Zebu staring back at me wide eyed through the side bars. I wondered if they saw the angel too. I think Igor must have seen her, because his mouth was hanging wide open like he was in shock.

I laid wide awake in bed, pondering everything that just happened to me for a couple hours before I finally drifted asleep.

******

I woke up the next morning expecting to see or feel some kind of miracle in my life, but when I gazed at my reflection in the mirror, my heart sank low. There wasn't any visible change in my appearance at all. Not even a little bit. I thought that I must have been dreaming about seeing an angel the night before.

I heard the visitors' shouting for me to come outside and show my face. A minute later I heard them chanting, "We want the monster! We want the monster! We want the monster!"

My feet dragged across the dirt to the cave opening. I saw parents, kids, and even grandparents with walking canes, rushing down the pathway to join the other three visitors already tormenting me. They hurried past the giraffe, rhinoceros and elephant exhibit. When they reached my exhibit, they leaned over the railing, stared across the moat, and shouted many hurtful words to me.

I saw a little girl tug on her mother's overcoat and cry out, "Where's the mushroom monster, Mommy? Where is she?"

An elderly couple said, "We paid good money to get in here. Where is that dreadful looking monster?" A man with his arm wrapped around his two boys' shoulders shouted, "My kids want to see the monster right now! They have two nice bags of vegetables to give her."

I thought, right, *more like rotten smelly food to throw at me*. Tears started to bead in my eyes. No one ever gave me a food gift that wasn't spoiled rotten, just like those kids.

I saw a lady holding a basket with a loaf of bread sticking part way out of it. I wished that someone would care enough to share a nice piece of bread like that with me. I felt so hungry.

The moment I stepped outside of my cave, I saw the zoo attendant shuffle people around and say, "Come on, come on, let everyone have a chance to see the mushroom monster. Don't be greedy now."

They yelled many unkind words at me, then, just like always, I had to brace myself.

Several kids pulled "rotten looking" veggies out from their paper bags. I raised my hands to try and block the assortment of food thrown at me.

One of the girls yelled out, "Mommy, I read about a monster in a book. Why don't they find a man monster, then they could have baby monsters, too."

I was so mad at that girl when I heard her say that.

The crowd grew even bigger, and their screams and shouts became too much for me to bear. Igor somehow knew that I was in extra pain and lured people away from my exhibit by walking across a tightrope to get their attention. Igor always seemed to do that special trick whenever he saw a large crowd of people making me feel sad.

CHAPTER 8

At the end of another long day of having to stand before a crowd of *mean* visitors, I was finally able to retire to my cave for the night. When I stepped in front of the mirror, I could hardly believe what I was seeing. There was more food splattered on my skin and clothes than I could ever remember in the past. I started to cry loud and hard. A couple minutes later, the most unusual thing happened. I saw Igor reach through the bars and drop a clump of red flowers into my cave. I walked over, picked them up, and inhaled their sweet fragrance. I just realized, at that very moment, that I was wrong thinking Higgins was the only one who loved or showed any compassion toward me. Igor must have heard me crying and gathered some wild flowers growing along the edge of his enclosure. Although I couldn't speak to thank him, I was still able to gesture with my hands how much I loved and appreciated his gift.

I looked at myself in the mirror again and found it hard to believe how extra ugly I looked that evening. Honestly, I thought I looked like a walking vegetable dump of rotten food. I just couldn't help it, and started crying again, so much, for such a long time, my face and body became wet from my tears. I cried harder than I ever did in my entire life, until there were no more tears to come out.

I saw Igor jumping up and down, beating his chest, and grunt like he could somehow feel my pain and wanted to help.

I felt totally exhausted, and after a few minutes fell fast asleep.

It was very hot and dry in the cave that evening, more so than I ever remembered in the past. I awakened in the middle of the night feeling something strange happening to my body. I got up, lit the lantern, and gazed at myself in the mirror. I was horrified at what I saw. My moldy skin had shrunk and cracked all over my body. My face appeared so wrinkled I could hardly believe it. I just couldn't stand to look at my ugly self any longer, so I grabbed at my monstrous face, and to my horror, a hand full of gray muck came off and stuck to my hands. My eyes stretched wide, and pulse quickened.

Oh my gosh, I thought. *Is my face is coming off?*

I feared that at any moment my face would be completely gone. I could not bear to see my reflection anymore, so I picked up a stone and threw it at the mirror, breaking it to pieces.

The noise from the shattered mirror must have startled Igor and Zebu awake because I saw them staring back at me with wide stretched eyes. I didn't think gorillas could show extreme emotion, but the instant Igor saw my face he screamed, jumped up and down and beat his chest. That same instant, Zebu darted out of sight like he was frightened by a strange new monster. I thought, *oh great, now I looked so horrible, even my two best friends are afraid to look at me.* Poor Igor and Zebu, they must have been shocked to see my face like this.

I leaned forward, feeling as if I was going to throw up, when a piece of broken mirror reflected something strange on the middle of my right cheek, about the size of a quarter. It looked like pure, unblemished skin. I quickly dipped my hand into the bucket of water and washed my cheek to expose more of the hidden skin. I just couldn't believe how soft it felt. It appeared to be normal, silky, even-colored, and beautiful.

I really got excited and started to wash my face faster and faster, all around my eyes, forehead, and neck, until the rest of the gray muck was gone. I raised the lantern close to my face, and once again looked at my reflection in the piece of mirror. I was shocked to see a beautiful girl staring back at me. She was like a stranger I never knew existed before. *Could it be she was hidden beneath my outer shell of ugliness for all these years, and I just never knew it?*

I saw beautiful, soft hair at my forehead where just moments ago I could only see a moldy looking mop. I quickly washed the rest of my hair in the bucket of water until all the muck came off. I looked at myself again and saw shiny, flowing hair, all the way down to my shoulder.

The water in my bucket turned dark and murky. I needed more clean water to wash off the rest of my body, so I ran outside to the edge of the moat and repeatedly splashed myself with water until all the remaining goo was gone. My entire body now appeared to be soft and beautiful, like the skin of a newborn baby. I rushed back into the cave just to make sure the beautiful girl was still there. I blinked over and over again, trying to shake off the reflection of the strange girl looking back at me, believing that she was just a dream, and that at any moment I would see my former hideous self in the mirror again. But to my delight, the image of the girl stayed with me.

The only blemish that remained was a very unusual black mole in the shape of a star on the inside of my right wrist.

When I looked back, I was shocked to see Igor raise his hand and give me the "V" for victory sign.

Feeling completely exhausted, I laid down on my bed and fell fast asleep.

CHAPTER 9

The following morning, I was jolted out of bed by the screams of visitors calling out to see me. I dragged my feet over to the cave opening and saw a crowd of twenty people already waiting for me to come out.

"Where is she? Where's the Mushroom Monster?" they asked.

A young mother held her daughter in her arms and shouted, "We paid good money to see her. She better show her ugly face, right now!"

"Better come out of your cave now, if you expect any supper tonight," said one of the zoo workers.

I stepped out into the morning light in a complete daze, expecting at any moment to hear the kids and adults scream at me, but this time it was different. I saw their mouths hanging open in complete silence. I wondered what they were thinking. I sensed fear in their faces, but of a different kind than I was used to seeing.

One of the mothers pointed at me and cried out, "There's a beautiful girl! A beautiful maid is trapped in the monster's cage! Help her, quick!"

A young boy shouted, "The mushroom child is going to get her! Hurry!"

I looked back toward the cave, wondering what they were talking about, then gazed down at my arms and legs and saw beautiful skin. *Was what happened to me the night before for real, and not a dream?* I pinched myself. Yes! Yes! It really must be true.

Of course they didn't know. They must be thinking my other self is still in the cave, about to come out and get me.

One of the dads quickly climbed over the fence, then dove into the moat, making a big splash. He swam across, climbed out, and ran up to me. "Don't worry," he said. "I won't let her get you."

Was he trying to rescue me from my former self? I thought, How weird was that?

His daughter cupped her hands around her mouth and shouted, "Daddy! Daddy! Hurry! The mushroom monster is in the cave! The Mushroom Monster is going to get you!" Her mom whisked her up into her arms and she quickly hid her face in her thick coat. The mom shouted, "I think she's coming! Hurry! Get her out! Fast!"

Before I knew it, the man swept me up into his arms and carried me toward the moat. He stopped at the edge of the water and looked back, probably expecting to see the Mushroom Monster rush out of the cave at any moment to try and get us.

I wrapped my arms around his neck and hung on for dear life as he swam across the moat. Next, he carried me get to the top of the fence where three other men were waiting to help me get safely down the other side.

The next thing I knew, I was laying in the middle of the zoo pathway with a crowd of people gathering around me. They leaned forward and stared down at me with worried expressions.

An elderly woman dropped her wooden cane, cupped her hands over her mouth and looked as if she was in shock after witnessing what happened.

I felt extremely weak and cold, not even having the strength to get back up. I turned my head and looked toward my cave exhibit. There she was, Miss Finch, running around the front grass area, looking for the Mushroom Monster. She shouted, "Come out you wretched beast! Where are you hiding this time?" She stood in the middle of grass area, placed her hands firmly on her hips, then slowly turned a circle. "You can't hide for long! Just wait until I get my hands on you!" She smiled at the crowd in silence a moment, then resumed her frantic search for the Mushroom Monster. She rushed around like crazy, searching all my past hiding places, including behind the boulders, trees, and bushes. She even looked in the moat to see if perhaps her precious monster might have drowned.

I knew all that she was going to find would be a pile of grey, moldy goop next to the shattered mirror in the cave.

Two young women knelt on each side of me and clasped my hands. "Don't worry," one woman said. "You'll be OK. You're safe now." The other said, "No monster can get you here."

A kindhearted woman rolled her wool sweater into a ball and placed it under my neck for a pillow. "How did you get in that dreadful cage, dear child?" she asked.

"What is your name?" asked another.

I gave them a blank stare, unable to respond.

A mother ran her hand softly back across my forehead. "The poor dear must be in shock. I bet that's why she can't speak."

I felt something I never felt before at that moment. People acted as if they really cared and were worried about me. It felt so good to be on the other side of the fence, away from the reflection of my former monster self.

A woman took off her boots and put them on my feet. It was wonderful to have my feet feel so warm. They even put a beautiful jacket on me. I could hardly believe all of their kindness. These were my first real clothes, and they felt so good to have on. They were wonderful gifts from people who thought they rescued me from the Mushroom Monster. If they only knew the truth, I bet they wouldn't believe it in a million years.

It was hard to believe how such a wonderful miracle could happen in my life. I felt like smiling for the first time ever.

They kept asking me who I was, where my parents were, and how I got trapped inside the monster exhibit. As hard as I tried to speak, I couldn't utter a single word.

I was so tired, and my eyes felt very heavy. Moments later I drifted sound asleep.

CHAPTER 10

When I finally woke up I discovered that I was in a nice bed covered with white sheets up to my neck. Miss Finch, a nurse, and a doctor stood at my bedside and talked about what happened to me back at the zoo.

Miss Finch waited until everyone had left the hospital room, then leaned over my bed and stared down at me with squinted eyes. "How? How did you get inside the Mushroom Monster exhibit?"

Before I had the chance to gesture with my hands that I couldn't speak, she walked over to the front door, looked up and down the hallway a moment, then quickly hurried back to me. "Come on! Speak up!" she continued to rant. "Tell me! How? How did you get inside the Mushroom Monster exhibit?" Her voice grew louder. "How did you get inside?"

I put my hand to my mouth to let her know that I couldn't speak.

She shook her head, looked the other way a moment, and then thrust her face back at me again. "Oh, don't play dumb with me. What happened to the mushroom girl? What did you do with her?"

I gestured with my hands and shook my head, trying to let her know that I couldn't answer back.

She put on a fake looking smile. "All I saw was a pile of moldy grey muck in front of a broken mirror; the same muck that was found on your clothes." She leaned up, placed her hands on her hips and stared down at me. "How did you get her clothes? Why did you put them on?"

I pointed at my mouth for the third time to try and convince her that I couldn't speak.

She stepped back, took a deep breath, then stared down at me in silence. "Another mute, I can't believe it! First the Mushroom Monster... and now you. I'll be getting the truth out of you, mute or no mute. Just you see."

She stared down at me in silence a moment. "No. You couldn't be," she said. "Couldn't be the same as... Impossible." Next, she grasped my arm and stared at the star-shaped mole on the side of my wrist. "What an odd mark."

******

A couple days later, Miss Finch brought me in her carriage to the Brunsville County Courthouse. Right before entering the front door, she grabbed my shoulder from behind and swung me around. "If you ever, ever, want to see your parents again, you better go along with everything I say from here on out, especially when we go before the judge. Got it?"

I nodded.

Miss Finch walked up to Judge Randall and offered him a big piece of chocolate. "Have one Judge."

The judge's eyes narrowed. "That wouldn't be a sweet bribe you're offering me, now would it?"

"Why... of course not. Just thought you'd like some chocolate." She smiled. "Everyone thinks you to be such a sweet judge."

******

Miss Finch spent the next hour in the courtroom office discussing my case before the judge. I don't know how, but she somehow managed to convince him to give her temporary custody of me until I was claimed by my rightful parents, or next of kin.

The judge said that posters of my picture

were already sent out to the nearby towns. I knew that it would be impossible for my parents to recognize me in my new body.

Miss Finch never stopped smiling and acted so sweet in front of me. I think she was just trying to impress the judge. I felt like pushing her back right then and there, but was afraid of what she said to me earlier about not getting to see my parents again. I felt she knew the truth about me and my former Mushroom Monster self, but couldn't get herself to fully believe it. Heck, I could hardly believe it either.

Miss Finch extended her hand to me and smiled, but I stepped back, keeping my arms close to my side. Judge Randall took note of my cold response and looked a little concerned.

"She's still in shock, and timid of everyone," said Miss Finch.

Judge Randall nodded. "That's to be expected."

She stepped toward the door with me at her side, then looked back over her shoulder. "Nothing to worry about, Judge Randall. I'll be taking good care of her until she is claimed by her rightful parents, or next of kin."

CHAPTER 11

Miss Finch told me to hurry up and get inside the carriage the moment we stepped out of the courtroom. I think she was worried that Judge Randall might change his mind at any moment about giving her temporary custody of me.

I felt her hand push against my back to rush me inside the carriage. "Come on. We don't have all day. We must hurry!"

The driver got the horses off to a fast gallop. I looked out of the carriage window and noticed that the door handle on my side was tied with a cord so it couldn't be opened.

Miss Finch looked down at me and grinned. "Don't even think about trying to get out," she smirked. "I'll be taking good care of you. You have nothing to be worried about."

After a long, bumpy ride, the carriage pulled up alongside a grey stone, two-story house, surrounded by green pastures. Bushy trees, ranging in color from deep green to bluish shades, spotted the landscape. I gazed out the carriage window and down to the valley below. Cows and sheep could be seen grazing upon vast fields of grass.

An elderly lady in a house directly across the street from us peeped out her window. Before I knew it, she stepped out the front door, then walked up to us wearing a bright yellow dress and feathered hat. "Gracious me," she said, giving us a big smile. "Who's your guest?"

I figured her neighbor didn't have much else to do, living out in the middle of nowhere, than inquire of every new person who crossed her path.

Miss Finch put on one of her fake smiles. "She was found in the zoo's Mushroom Monster exhibit."

The lady put her hand over her mouth. "Gracious me! The Mushroom Monster exhibit? Dreadful. Simply dreadful!"

Miss Finch grinned and put her arm around my shoulder. "Judge Randall gave me temporary custody of her until we find her lawful parents, or next of kin. I have a lovely room waiting inside, just for her." She turned and gave me another fake smile. "I think she'll love it."

As we headed toward the front door, a cockroach suddenly raced across the path in front of us. That same instant, Miss Finch jumped back. "Dreadful, filthy, vile creatures!" she screeched. "If there's anything I can't stand, it's a creepy cockroach."

CHAPTER 12

The moment I stepped into Miss Finch's house I saw fancy furnishings everywhere. I couldn't wait to see my bedroom, and wondered what kind of food I would be getting to eat.

She led me upstairs, down the hallway, and into a beautifully decorated bedroom. On both sides of the window were several dolls, each having a unique face and wearing a different colored dress. I loved the interesting stitch designs on their clothes.

Miss Finch put her arm around my shoulder and gave me a big smile. "Ah yes, I can see the sparkle in your eye." She turned and spread her arms far apart. "Isn't this room simply a dream come true?"

I nodded and grinned. *Oh my gosh*, I thought, was this beautiful bedroom set aside just for me? Everything looked so clean and well kept. This room would be just perfect for me.

She showed me some paintings hanging on the wall, including one of her daughter riding a blue bicycle. A bouquet of red and white roses filled the bike's front basket. I wondered if her daughter might be a musician, because she had a guitar strapped to her back.

I smiled, admiring a watercolor painting of two cats dressed in human clothes, one in a blue dress, the other in a black suit. They faced each other in a flower garden with a picnic basket filled with milk bottles at their side.

Everything about the room seemed to be perfect, I thought, *perhaps I was wrong about Miss Finch after all.*

At that moment, when I was feeling so very happy, something happened that took all my joy away. She squinted and wagged her finger at me. "I don't want you, ever, ever to step foot in this, or my other daughter's bedroom. Understand?"

I nodded as if I understood, but actually I didn't. If her daughters were gone, what would it matter if I got to stay in one of their rooms?

Her eyes narrowed. "Just so you know, my daughters insist that everything be left perfect, just the way they left it, for when they come to visit me once a year."

My heart sank low in disappointment. *This can't be true.*

She had me follow her down the hallway, then step into a room that was completely bare, with the exception of a small round wall mirror having a rusted frame, and a bed without a cushion. There were just grey bed sheets covering a plank of wood, just like back at the cave.

Miss Finch grinned. "What you're looking at is all I got as an orphan child; a hard bed, and that same mirror. No one ever gave me anything good growing up. Do you think you are better than me, or deserve more?"

I sighed, then shook my head.

Miss Finch swiped her hand down across the wall's surface, then showed me her fingertips. "See, I personally dusted this nice storage room before you arrived. Aren't you lucky? Isn't it roomy?"

How could this be? I looked around the room. There wasn't even a window to get some fresh air. It was almost as dreary as the zoo cave. I turned and looked at her, and thought, *you greedy person. You must be kidding me.* Her selfish way made me all the more want to find a way to escape from her home.

Miss Finch smiled. "Every square foot of this

house is precious to me. I need all the comforts for me and my daughters for when they come back to visit."

My hands curled into a fist.

"Child, don't ever make a fist at me, that is, if you know what's good for you. I might decide not to give you any more chocolate pieces if you do that again. Wouldn't that be simply dreadful? Chocolate makes everyone so sweet. Don't you think so?"

I thought, *you don't even know the meaning of sweet, chocolate or no chocolate.* I tried to remember what Higgins taught me about being thankful for what we have, even in times of grief. This was definitely one of those times.

I thought, at least it isn't too cold in the storage room, and I didn't have anyone throwing food at me, like back at the zoo.

CHAPTER 13

Miss Finch led me downstairs and into her living room. I saw a brown leather couch and red velvet sofa having two large purple pillows at each end. Behind the sofa were four shelves packed with all kinds of books of different sizes and colors.

There were three clay pots sitting on a desk by the windowsill. The soil had a thick layer of green moss growing on top. In the center of each pot was a miniature trellis having a leafy green vine with tiny orange trumpet flowers.

Miss Finch's face suddenly turned mean looking. "My, what a brave girl you were, going into the cave with the monster like that."

I thought, *Oh no, is she going to talk about that again?*

She stepped closer. "Come now, spit it out. Where is the monster? Did you bury her?"

I gestured with my hands that I couldn't answer her.

"Well, if you're going to stay here with me, you must have a name. Since you can't speak for yourself, and the Mushroom Monster has seemed to have vanished into thin air, I'll call you by her first name." She pointed at me. "From now on, your name is Hailee. Any complaints?"

I shook my head, and was actually very happy to have her call me by my real name.

She reached out and gripped my shoulder. Her large white hands felt cold, just like everything else about her. "Well, until your parents arrive, if they "*ever*" do, you will work here for "*me*," and "*earn*" every penny of your keep. Understand?"

I nodded.

She clenched her hands into a tight fist. "You're going to work. That means cooking meals, and cleaning house." She tilted her head to one side and stared at me in silence a moment. "You are a strange one. Well, you'll certainly have your work cut out for you here." She reached out and grabbed my wrists. "Let me see your hands." Her eyes narrowed. "Smooth as a baby. Just as I thought. I suppose you haven't worked a day in your life, have you?"

I gave her a blank stare.

"Well... the first thing you do when you get up in the morning is make my breakfast. I gather you don't know how to properly cook eggs either, do you?"

I shook my head.

She gave me a sneer. "Well… you're not going to get out of work by being ignorant in this house. I'll show you how. Never forget, I like a dozen eggs, sunny side up, each and *every* morning. And if you should happen to break one of the yolks," she squinted and lightly tapped her finger upon my chest, "you're going to pay by *not* getting any lunch or supper for the whole day. Understand?"

I nodded.

Miss Finch repeatedly opened and closed her hands. "So you better have strong hands, and at the same time, nimble fingers, for cooking eggs and scrubbing floors." She gazed at my clothes while shaking her head. "No, no, no, those will never do." She fetched some ordinary looking clothes and handed them to me. "I want you to wear these while living here."

I was so disgusted with the ugly looking clothes she gave me. I felt like tossing them onto the floor in front of her black boots. I could hardly stand to look at the plain brown, long-sleeve shirt, and full length pants, the same boring color.

She reached into her side pocket and handed me a piece of chocolate. "Here, have one. Bet you never met anyone as sweet as me." She smiled. "Now, this is something to dream about. Besides getting free chocolate pieces; if you really work hard I might even consider making you like a stepdaughter."

More like slave-daughter, I thought. Instead of having to wax her precious floor, I felt like waxing the top of her head with melted chocolate.

Miss Finch grinned. "Are you thinking about something... sweet?"

I gave her a big nod, and smiled. Being mute had the advantage of making me hold my tongue, so I couldn't give her a piece of my mind. Higgins taught me that we're not perfect beings. I guessed I needed to work on thinking kinder thoughts, even in the presence of unkind souls.

******

I followed Miss Finch's lead out of the living room and into the kitchen. The grey ceiling had thick wood beams, spread about three feet apart. The walls were painted white, and over a foot thick.

To the back of the kitchen, sitting on a shelf above the brick fireplace were five ceramic plates, each one having pictures of climbing roses glazed onto the surface. I saw several cooking utensils hanging on hooks on either side of the fireplace, including six copper pots of different sizes.

In the middle of the room was a large brass ceiling lamp hanging above the kitchen table.

I was startled to see a huge cockroach lying on its back at the far corner of the kitchen. It was the biggest bug I've ever seen in my entire life. Instead of scaring Miss Finch with it, which at the moment I didn't think was a bad idea, I used the edge of my shoe to slide the dead bug out of sight under the cabinet ledge.

I looked behind me and saw a shiny red door by the side of the kitchen with stacks of boxes in front of it.

Miss Finch quickly stepped between me and the red door, blocking my view. "Oh, so you're curious about that door, and what might be inside the room, are you?"

I nodded.

She gave me a grin. "Wonder why those boxes are in front of the door?"

I nodded.

"Well, don't. That room is strictly *off limits!* Never go in there! Understand?"

I nodded.

She pointed at the top box. "That's where I keep my precious cocoa powder. The other boxes are filled with cleaning supplies. You'll need lots of them while living here."

I leaned to one side and tried to get another look at the red door, but she quickly stepped in front of me and blocked my view again.

I walked to the far side of the kitchen and looked out a large window having a beautiful view of a flower garden. The scene reminded me of one of Higgins's paintings.

I felt a sudden tap on my back shoulder.

"Are you a daydreamer?" she asked, squinting at me with one eye. "Let's make one thing perfectly clear; I don't tolerate daydreamers in this house. Understand?"

I nodded.

"Good." She pointed out the window toward her barn. "First thing in the morning, after feeding the chickens, cleaning the barn, and preparing my dozen eggs for breakfast, I want you to scrub the floor in the living room. I want it waxed and polished. Understand?" She squinted at me. "If I can't see my reflection on the wood floor, it will cost you your dinner. Understood?"

I nodded. Now I knew why there were so many cracks in the floor. The wood probably couldn't stand her reflection.

******

I kind of enjoyed waking up early in the morning to feed the chickens and collect the eggs for breakfast, but hated to think about what might happen to me, or any one of the chickens if they should happen to come up short of her daily dozen eggs. I might get stuck without lunch and dinner, but the poor chicken would probably end up becoming Miss Finch's lunch or dinner.

I always had to be on guard while tossing feed to the chickens, because a huge white goose named Jenny Ann, loved to sneak up when I wasn't looking and give me a nip in the behind. Next, she would stretch her long white neck at me and flap her orange beak, making the most annoying honking sounds. It was so nerve racking. I very much disliked Jenny Ann.

******

I was given strict orders whenever I prepared or served her any food or drink to put on my cook's outfit; a full-length white apron, and tall white hat.

"This is how I want my vegetables prepared," she said, putting several potatoes, tomatoes, carrots, and stalks of celery on the cutting board. She started dicing them into small cubes. "See, like this. Not big pieces. Not small pieces. Just right. Got it?"

I nodded.

Her eyes narrowed. "Are you sure?"

I nodded again.

Sometimes, when I looked over her shoulder while watching her give instructions on how to cook, I would place my hands firmly on my hips, give her a sneer, and think to myself, *you got to be kidding.*

When she looked back at me I quickly dropped my arms to my side and smiled sweetly. When she looked away, I put my hands back on my hips again. I liked to play that game with her. Good thing I never got caught. I sometimes wondered if she suspected I was acting silly behind her back because quite often she would turn around really fast as if trying to catch me doing something.

I experienced many smells in my life, most very unpleasant, but the ones in Miss Finch's kitchen, to the contrary, were quite delightful to the senses. She taught me many interesting and sweet recipes. I associated the smells with food names like gingerbread, angel cake, and blueberry muffins. I couldn't ever imagine anyone having a bigger sweet tooth than Miss Finch. Unfortunately, all that food did nothing to make her the least bit sweeter. I thought devil's food cake and sourdough bread might be foods that would better match her personality.

The amount of food I served her in a single meal was more than I got to eat in an entire month when I lived at the zoo. She loved to eat lots and lots of large juicy steaks. I often wondered where she went to get so much meat. I didn't think a stomach could hold that much food all at once. I couldn't get the image out of my mind, seeing her stuff her face like that.

I thought that it would be so nice to sit at a table and to have as much food as I wanted to eat like she did, but I never complained, nor could I, even if I wanted to.

******

I stepped into Miss Finch's bedroom, just like I did every night, and served her a cup of hot cocoa with an added half-teaspoon of her sleeping medicine. She normally requested that I add a whole teaspoon, but she said she felt very tired that night and only needed a half dose.

I waited outside the bedroom for her to fall

asleep. After she started to snore, I tiptoed down the hallway and entered one of her daughters' bedrooms. I knew she didn't want me to go in the room, but I just couldn't resist cradling one of the dolls. I thought, *it wouldn't hurt anything, and besides, it would be so nice to know how it feels to hold one of those beautiful dolls in my arms.*

I was drawn to the large doll with the red velvet dress. I picked her up and held her eye level, admiring all the details that made her appear so lifelike. I looked around at all the furnishings and felt so much at peace being in such a beautiful room.

I was startled by the sound of the door slamming shut behind me.

Miss Finch shouted, "How dare you step foot in my daughter's bedroom!"

She caught me red handed, she did, holding one of her daughters' prized dolls.

Her large feet stomped up to me. "Didn't I tell you to stay out of this bedroom, and especially not to touch anything?" She leaned forward, then put her mouth close to my ear. "Are you daft? Didn't you hear me before?"

She snatched the doll out from my hands and tossed it onto the bed. "Now, go to your room this instant!" she said, pointing out the door. "You're lucky to have such a nice place to sleep, not to mention getting "*free*" food and wonderful bits of sweet chocolate for doing just a "*little*" bit of chores."

I thought, yeah, right, a little bit of chores from morning to night, scrubbing the floors, washing dishes, cleaning carpets, cooking food, dusting the house, feeding the chickens, and not to mention, getting nipped in the behind by her honkin' goose, Jenny Ann.

******

I was still very upset at Miss Finch the following evening for the cruel way she frightened me for going into her daughter's bedroom, so decided to get teach her a lesson. I went into the kitchen and found the monster cockroach I discovered the first day I arrived, then picked it up and slid it into my side pocket. Next, I sneaked upstairs while Miss Finch was busy reading one of her books in the living room.

I looked about her bedroom, trying to think of a nice place to put the dead bug. *Ah yes,* I thought, focusing on her bed. I gently placed Mr. Cockroach on the pillow to make it look like it was sleeping on its back. Next, I pulled the cover half way up over its body so its head and first few legs were plainly visible.

About a half hour later, I heard a very loud scream while I was busy cleaning the kitchen. *Yep, I thought, I bet she found Mr. Cockroach.*

"Hailee! Hailee!" she shouted in a panicked tone of voice. "Come here! Quick!"

I ran upstairs and into the bedroom. Miss Finch was leaning back against the dresser with all the color drained from her face, and it looked like she was shaking.

"Get it out! Get it out!" she shouted, pointing at the bed.

I pretended I didn't see anything, and gestured that I didn't know what was wrong.

She stepped closer to the bed, pointing at the giant cockroach. "Can't you see it?" Her neck stretched forward, squinting in the direction of the cockroach. **"IT'S DADDY GOOSE BUMP! HE'S COME BACK FROM THE DEAD AND SLEEPING IN MY BED! I CAN'T BELIEVE IT!"** She snapped her head at me, then looked back toward the cockroach. "Can't you see him?" She took three steps toward the bed and pointed again. "There! There he is! Are you blind?"

Poor Daddy Goose Bump, I thought. He appeared to be resting so peacefully. I thought it to be such a shame to disturb him.

After repeated pleas to get him out of her bed, I finally took Daddy Goose Bump outside and gave him a proper burial for helping me teach Miss Finch a lesson.

******

I looked over my long list of cleaning chores the next morning and sighed. How she expected me to do so much cleaning in one day was beyond my wildest imagination.

The next thing I knew, I found myself kneeling down and polishing her precious floor for over an hour. I felt very tired and decided to sit down on the living room couch to get a well-deserved moment's rest. My timing was bad, because a minute later, Miss Finch entered the room and caught me slouching on her couch. Her nostrils flared, and face reddened. "Well, well, well!" she said, swaying her head from side to side. "Isn't this a pretty sight! Napping on my favorite couch, are you?"

She looked back at the clock, then toward me again. "By the way, I don't want to seem to be too unkind, but you've been just a tad bit "too lazy" today and behind on your list of other cleaning chores." She walked up to me, then squinted down at the floor in front of my feet. "I'm sure you can do a much better job at waxing the floor than that. Why, I can hardly see my reflection at all."

I thought, *Why don't you look into a real mirror, Miss Finch?*

"Don't doddle," she said. "Now get up and get busy. You'll find out, soon enough, that slackers get little to eat in my house."

CHAPTER 14

Miss Finch acted very strange the moment she got back home from the zoo on Mondays and Fridays. She would park the carriage, look in every direction to make sure she wasn't being watched, then step into the carriage and shut the door behind her. When she stepped out seconds later, it appeared as if she was hiding something beneath her coat. Next, she would slip in through the back kitchen door, lock it, and then immediately lock the other door too, the one leading to the hallway. There was no way for me to peep inside to see what she was doing in there. When she came out of the kitchen a short time later, it appeared as if whatever she had beneath her coat wasn't there anymore. I knew she was hiding something in the kitchen, and was determined to find out exactly what it was.

******

On Friday afternoon, I knew Miss Finch wouldn't be back from the zoo for quite some time. Three large sacks of potatoes were delivered to the house the day before. I emptied one of the bags, hid myself inside, then cut a small hole in the burlap so I could peek out.

I heard the back kitchen door open and close, then saw Miss Finch enter the room. I could tell that she was hiding something beneath her coat again. She walked up to the red door, slid the boxes aside, then entered the room.

It seemed like an eternity for her to come back out again. I felt very nervous, and knew that if she caught me in the potato sack I would be in big trouble. I heard the door squeak open and watched her step out. There she was... in her normal size again. Now I knew her secret hiding place. I put my finger to my chin and thought, *I wonder what she's hiding in there?* It must be something important, or she wouldn't be trying so hard to keep it a secret.

Miss Finch left the kitchen and headed down

the hallway toward the living room. I gasped when I heard her shout, "Hailee! Hailee! Where are you?"

I jumped out of the potato sack, then ran out the back kitchen door to the chicken coop.

A minute later, I saw Miss Finch step outside the back door and stare at me.

"Oh, so you forgot to feed the chickens this morning, did you? Well, hurry up and get back inside."

I took a deep breath, feeling relieved that I didn't get caught. Now I knew *"where"* she was hiding something. Next, I was determined to find out *"what"* it was.

******

The next morning, after serving breakfast, I handed Miss Finch her black coat by the front door. Just As she was about to step outside, she stopped and looked back at me. "Oh... by the way, you did remember how to make my Shepherd's Pie, didn't you?"

I nodded.

"Good, and don't forget to add the extra pound of meat I left on the kitchen table. When I get back, I expect my supper ready and waiting. Got it?"

I nodded.

"And don't make a mistake on the recipe, or else."

I stepped into the kitchen and began preparing her special dinner. As I started to slice and dice the potatoes and carrots into small cubes, I glanced over my shoulder at the red door. I thought, *Now would be a good time to see what Miss Finch might be hiding in there.*

I stepped outside the house and gazed down the road just to make sure she was gone, then rushed back into the kitchen and slid the boxes away from the red door. I felt my heart pound in my chest as I entered the room. It appeared to be empty inside, with the exception of a large freezer box. That's it, I thought, *Whatever she's hiding must be inside that box.* I saw red stains on the cement floor in front of it. They didn't look like paint. I got down on my hands and knees to get a closer look. *Oh no!* I thought. *The stains looked like dried blood!* I took a deep swallow. Dare I look inside? Will I have nightmares for the rest of my life after seeing what's in there?

I headed for the door, but then stopped and looked back over my shoulder. Perhaps there was a zoo animal in there. I felt like I had to protect the other animals at the zoo, so I stepped up to the freezer box, then reached down and gripped the edge of the metal lid. It felt cold to the touch and sent shivers up my spine. I took a deep breath and thought, *OK, on the count of three.* One…Two… Three. The instant I raised the lid and looked inside my eyes bulged wide in shock. I saw, perhaps, two hundred raw steaks packed in ice. I crossed my arms across in front of me and thought, *Now I know why Miss Finch was starving the animals. She was stealing the zoo's meat to fill her own belly!* It's no wonder she asked me to cook steaks for her nearly every night, and stuff her Shepherd's Pie with so much extra meat. Only someone like her could do such a horrible thing as starve an animal to fill her own belly. I felt an urgent need to take action and figure out a plan to rescue my dear friend Zebu before it was too late.

I slipped into the kitchen and put the boxes back in front of the red door, just the way I found them. My hands felt shaky, but I was still able to finish making her dinner.

Later in the day, I heard the front door open and close, then Miss Finch's unmistakable footsteps heading toward the kitchen. Thump, thump, thump. They grew louder with every second. I stood by the kitchen table, next to her two-pound Shepherd's Pie.

She stopped at the entranceway and stared into the kitchen. "Well, it's a good thing you got my Shepherd's Pie done in time. You better have prepared it according to my *"exact"* instructions."

She was about to take a bite when she suddenly stopped and stared at the boxes stacked in front of the red door. Next, she leaned across the table and squinted at me in silence. "You haven't been doing any snooping around lately... have you?"

I felt very nervous that moment, worried that I didn't put the boxes back exactly the way she left them.

She quickly got up and walked over to the boxes, then looked back at me with a mean look.

I thought, *Oh no. She knows. Should I run?*

"Just as I thought," she shouted.

She slowly turned and looked back at me. "Come here!"

I felt so nervous, I didn't think I couldn't move.

She pointed at me and demanded, "Come here!"

I forced myself to walk up to her.

"Didn't I tell you...?" she started to say.

I was expecting her to accuse me of going inside her secret room. I looked toward the back door and thought about making a run for it, but instead took a deep sigh of relief when I heard her finish the rest of her sentence.

"Didn't I tell you to let me know when we got low on cocoa so I could order more? It takes two weeks to get a new shipment in. Can't you remember anything?"

I took a deep breath, feeling so relieved that she didn't notice any of the boxes were moved.

CHAPTER 15

I waited until Miss Finch was sound asleep, then slipped out the back kitchen door and into the night. I needed to find a place to hide my friend Zebu for when the time came for me to try to rescue him from the zoo.

After searching for about thirty minutes, I discovered what appeared to be an abandoned horse stable. The two side windows were broken and covered with spider webs. The hinges to the front gate were so rusted I was barely able to get it open. Looking up, I saw a black horse weathervane. Gazing to my right I saw two carriage wheels leaning against the side wall with their rusted metal bands laying on the dirt in front of them. There were two horseshoes nailed to the front door.

When I entered the barn, I saw four horse stalls and a large leather saddle covered thick in dust. I thought, *This would be the perfect place to hide Zebu.* All it needed was a little cleaning up.

I figured that the only way to rescue Zebu would be for me to drive the carriage to the zoo late one night, free him, then bring him back to this barn. I was already trained on how to hitch the horse to the carriage, and felt I stood a decent chance at being able to drive it to the zoo. My main concern was that Misty, the carriage horse, was very particular as to who was doing the driving. I decided to do some extra nice things for Misty to get on her good side so she would allow me to drive the carriage.

For the whole next week, I sneaked out late at night and pampered Misty by giving her extra apples and carrots. She liked it when I brushed her mane around the neck and hind legs. I treated her like royalty, and even filed her hoofs, which was quite a chore.

After a week of pampering, I was fairly certain that Misty would allow me to drive the carriage to the zoo. All I had to do now was set the second half of my plan in motion, and that was to decide on a day and time to get my friend Zebu out of the zoo.

CHAPTER 16

The night I planned to rescue Zebu had finally arrived. I felt excited, but at the same time nervous, not knowing for sure if everything would go according to plan. My biggest concern was that Miss Finch might not stay asleep the whole night and find me, Misty, and the carriage missing.

Just like every evening before, I filled Miss Finch's mug with boiling hot water, then stirred in a scoop of her cocoa powder, together with her sleeping medicine.

I headed upstairs and stopped for a moment just outside her bedroom door to practice my not-so-happy look, just like I always did right before entering her room. I knew that if I acted too happy or sad she might get suspicious and start asking questions. I couldn't afford to have anything go wrong on this night.

OK, here I go, I thought, heading into her bedroom. Miss Finch turned her head in bed and stared at me squinty eyed. "You did add my sleeping medicine tonight, didn't you?"

I nodded, and thought, *Yes I did Miss Finch, may you rest in peace, witch.* There I go again, thinking bad thoughts. I needed to remember what Higgins taught me about having patience and forgiveness for others, even if they may be your worst enemy. And I had to admit that Miss Finch was at the top of my list.

As hard as it was to be completely forgiving, I knew Higgins was right, because I always felt a great inner peace after getting rid of any hatred toward anyone.

Miss Finch wagged her finger at me. "You better have measured everything just right, or you're not going to get any food tomorrow... Did you hear me?"

I nodded and curtseyed, just like she taught me. My thoughts were so focused on the night's rescue plan, even Miss Finch's nasty voice didn't seem to bother me that much. After she finished sipping the last of her cocoa, I took the cup from her hand and gave her a last goodnight smile before heading out of the bedroom.

I stood outside her room and placed my ear up against the door. Just like clockwork, about five minutes later, she started to snore like a giant pig. I hoped and prayed that I could get to the zoo and back again before she woke up.

I headed downstairs, through the hallway and into the kitchen. Next, I entered Miss Finch's secret steak room. I decided to take one piece of meat to coax Zebu out of his cage, and another one to get him to follow me back up to the barn. Before I closed the lid to the freezer, I placed a piece of wood beneath a couple steaks to prop them up even with the other pieces of meat to make it look like nothing was missing.

I slipped out the back door, hitched Misty to the carriage, and stepped up onto the driver seat. The moment I gave the reins a light jingle, Misty started to trot down the road.

It was a perfect evening for the rescue, with a full moon to light the way before me. I figured Misty probably traveled this same road hundreds of times before, so I let her follow her instincts, and only gave little direction by pulling the reins to the left or right when we had to go around a curve in the road.

When the carriage neared the bottom of the

hill, I jingled the reins again, and was able to get Misty to go from a trot to a fast gallop. We passed by beautiful green pastures, thickets of holly bushes, and tall pines.

After traveling for several miles, I took a deep sigh of relief seeing the zoo finally appear in the distance. I was able to get Misty to turn down the back service road and stop across from the tiger exhibit. I stepped down from the carriage and gave her a big hug and kiss for helping me get to the zoo safe and sound.

I found Miss Finch's extra set of keys she kept hidden under the wooden crate by the storage shed.

The moment I opened the cage and stepped inside, Zebu scampered deep within the cave. His yellow eyes glowed back at me from the shadows, and he started to growl. I took out one of the steaks from my paper bag and held it out in front of him. To my delight, he followed me out of the cage and up to the carriage, never letting the steak get out of his sight. I tossed the piece of meat into the carriage and he leaped right in after it.

I was so worried about him because he appeared to be too thin, and looked like he was almost starving. I locked the cage and put the keys back under the wooden crate. I found a shovel and dug a hole under the iron bars to Zebu's cage to make it look like someone had tried to steal the tiger, or that the tiger clawed a big enough hole to get out. It was a good thing Zebu wasn't too big yet, or I would have had to spend a lot more time digging a bigger hole.

I looked toward the gorilla exhibit and saw Igor staring back at me, waving his hands above his head, trying to get my attention. He looked as if he wanted me to take him too. I walked up to my dear friend and stuck my hand through the bars, then touched fingertips, just like we did when we first became friends. I smiled and gestured with my hands to try to let him know that I loved him very much. I saw tears bead down his face. I wished I could take him too, but I knew it would be impossible to hide and feed the both of them. The instant I stepped up onto the carriage seat I heard Igor make a loud grunt. I looked back and was surprised to see him raise his hand and give me the "V" for victory sign. I thought that was so nice of him, even if he might not know what the "V" sign really stood for.

CHAPTER 17

As soon as I made it back to Miss Finch's house, I opened the carriage door and coaxed my tiger friend up the hill and into barn with another steak.

His coat was like a furry blanket and helped keep me warm that chilly night. I rubbed his neck and stroked my hand back across the top of his head while watching him fill his stomach with the juicy steak. He made a deep and mighty purr; the purr of a future beastly king whom I somehow wished ruled over man, because man could oft times be so cruel, so unkind, worst of all the beasts of the Earth. I kept him company for as long as it dare into the night, worried that Miss Finch might wake up at any moment and not find me in bed. I kissed Zebu's forehead and gave him one last goodnight hug before heading back down the road to Miss Finch's house.

******

I knew the exact moment when Miss Finch came home from work the following day when I heard the front door slam shut.

I leaned to one side and peered down the hallway toward the living room. I was shocked to see objects flying through the air, then crash and break against the walls and floor. Her rage could only mean one thing; she must have discovered Zebu was missing from the zoo.

She flashed into view at the opposite end of the hallway and stared back at me with bulging eyes. "I can't believe it!" she shouted, raising her hands high above her head. Her normally white cheeks were now beet red. "Someone stole the tiger cub!" She placed her hands firmly on her hips, took a couple deep breaths, then leaned toward me and grimaced. "What kind of monster would break into the zoo and steal the tiger?" She stomped over to the opposite end of the hallway where I was standing, then placed her face up to mine. "Do you have any idea who would do such a horrible thing?"

I looked at her with a blank expression on my face. It was a good thing I couldn't speak, because

Higgins taught me the importance of always telling the truth, even if it might hurt, and this would have hurt a lot. After two hours of screaming, she plopped onto her brown leather couch and stared out the window in silence.

******

After Miss Finch fell asleep each night, I would head up to the barn to fed Zebu and clean his straw bedding. It was a lot of extra work, but I didn't seem to mind it too much, because it was a sacrifice for one of God's splendid creatures I loved so dearly.

I didn't know if tigers could smile or not, but each evening, after I brought him a nice juicy steak from Miss Finch's freezer, he appeared to be so happy. He could hardly wait for the steaks to thaw out enough so he could devour them.

I kept Zebu company for about one to two hours every visit. With each steak removed from the freezer, I added another piece of wood beneath the other meats to make it look like nothing was missing. I knew that I could only fool Miss Finch for so long before she would discover the missing steaks, but that was a chance I was willing to take, and hoped before she found out I would have another plan put into action.

I managed to keep Zebu hidden for four weeks now. He grew fast and gained a lot of muscle thanks to all the extra steaks I fed him. I noticed also that his purr was getting deeper, louder, and mightier.

I had to be more careful about how my face looked in front of Miss Finch, because she was beginning to ask me why I looked happier than usual, even while scrubbing the floors or washing the dishes. I think it bothered her to be around anyone who didn't look or act as miserable as herself.

Three evenings later, my worst fears happened. I heard Zebu's growl echo down from the barn toward the house. I jumped up from the living room sofa and rushed over to shut the window.

I thought, *What am I going to do?* Miss Finch never goes to bed this early. If I didn't get to Zebu in a hurry to calm him down, he'll sure to be heard. I couldn't risk getting his steak yet. The last thing in the world I wanted would be for Miss Finch to hear his growl. I wouldn't even want to think about what might happen to me or Zebu if she discovered us hiding out in the barn.

I knew that she was upstairs in her bedroom.

Thank goodness the night was cold, and her window was probably shut. I decided to take a chance and head up to the barn early.

I slipped out the back kitchen door and walked up the hill as fast as I could. When I reached the barn door, I looked back over my shoulder and was shocked at what I saw. Miss Finch was staring back at me from the bottom of the hill with a very nasty look on her face.

Her mouth suddenly opened wide. "What are you doing up there, Hailee?" she shouted. She stomped up the hill, then stopped six feet in front of me. "Again I'm asking you! What are you doing up here by the barn?" Her eyebrows lowered. "I could hardly imagine you to be sleepwalking this early in the evening. What is it? Come on... confess?"

I gestured to her with my hands, like, *I don't know.*

She pointed at me and said, "Come here!"

The moment I walked up to her, she reached out and gripped the side of my shoulder, then dragged me to the barn door. "I'm asking you again. What are you doing up here?" She looked back and forth between me and the barn. "Are you hiding something in there? Is that it?"

I feared greatly for Zebu that moment, and

101

prayed Miss Finch wouldn't go inside. When she reached out for the door, I felt my heart drop in despair. I didn't know what to do.

She yanked the door open, expecting to find something. I looked inside and couldn't believe it. Zebu was smart enough to hide by himself. I bet he recognized her voice and remembered the whip. I knew he was hiding in one of the horse stalls, but which one? I saw his eyes flash at me from the stall at the far end. I hoped and prayed she didn't see him.

Miss Finch lit the lantern and said, "Well now, let's see what's so important for you to go sneaking up here at this time of night." She ordered me to hold the lantern out in front of her as she searched the first stall. She poked around the hay with a pointed stick for a moment, but found nothing. She had me to hold the lantern for her while she searched the second stall, then the third.

Finally, she approached the last stall where I knew Zebu was hiding. I had to think of something fast. I pretended to trip, and let the lantern slip from my fingers. When it hit the ground, the glass casing shattered, and the flame sparked a fire in the hay.

"Clumsy fool!" she said, grabbing a horse

blanket to smother the fire. She shook her head at me. "Do you want to burn down the whole barn?"

She dragged me by the shoulder down the road toward the house. "You're getting to be more trouble than you're worth; first the missing Mushroom Monster, and now the tiger."

She leaned forward until the tip of our noses almost touched. "If I didn't promise the judge to watch over you, I would throw you out into the street right this minute!" She pointed down the road. "Perhaps if you had to fend for yourself, and scrounge around in other peoples' trash for food, you would better appreciate all the good things I've done for you. Do you think for one moment it's easy for me to entertain strangers?"

I thought, *Do you think it's easy for me to entertain your house by slaving over it hand and foot to keep it clean?* I felt like I could endure her cruel words and twisted thoughts, because what was most important to me at that moment was Zebu's safety. I just wondered how much longer I could keep the secret going.

CHAPTER 18

When I entered the bedroom the next evening to give Miss Finch her cup of hot cocoa mixed with sleeping medicine, I noticed that her eyes were closed. I thought, *Did she pass away*? I placed her cocoa on the side dresser, then reached out and lightly tapped her shoulder.

I must have startled her, because her arm flew straight out and knocked her drink off the dresser table. I lunged forward to try to catch it as it fell, but her cocoa ended up spilling across the carpet.

He eyes bulged. "Look what you made me do! You should know better than to startle me like that! What's the matter with you? Have you lost your senses?" She pointed at the carpet. "Now clean up that mess, and get out!"

I hurried downstairs to get some cleaning rags in the kitchen, then rushed back to her bedroom and got down on my hands and knees to blot up the stains. I tried to ask her by making hand movements if she wanted me to get her another cup of cocoa with her sleeping medicine, but she shook her head and swiped her hand at me. "Don't bother! I'm very tired and don't need it tonight!"

I had to get out and feed Zebu shortly, but felt afraid to do so with Miss Finch still awake, and not having her sleeping medicine. I headed downstairs and tried to decide what to do next.

About ten minutes later, my worst fears happened when I heard Zebu's growls echo down from the barn. I was fearful that Miss Finch wasn't asleep yet and would hear him. I exchanged glances between the kitchen and the upstairs bedroom, and thought, *What shall I do now?* If I didn't get Zebu his steak quickly, Miss Finch would surely hear him. I didn't have any choice. I had to get him a steak, and do it fast. I hurried into the kitchen, slid the boxes away from the red door, then rushed over and opened the freezer. My hands felt shaky. The steak I was holding slipped through my fingers onto the floor, making a loud thud. I flashed my head back toward the kitchen door. *Thank goodness,* she was nowhere in sight.

I rushed out of the room, then quickly slid the boxes back in front of the door. Before heading out of the kitchen, I stopped and stared through the hallway toward the living room. It was all clear. I didn't know why, but I had this strange feeling come over me, like I was being watched. I ran up the hill to the barn as fast as my legs could carry me. Zebu quieted down the instant I gave him his steak. I stepped back to the barn door and stared down the road toward the house. Miss Finch was nowhere in sight.

I sat in front of Zebu and watched him eat. I wished I could explain to him that he must stay quiet if I'm a little late in bringing him his meat. I stroked my hand back across his head and listened to him purr. Three minutes into his meal he suddenly stopped eating in the middle of a bite. *That's weird,* I thought. He never stopped to take a break from eating like that before. He didn't look at me, but instead stared over my shoulder toward the barn door. I wondered what was making him act like that.

Next, his teeth clamped down so hard on the steak it sliced in half and dropped at his feet.

The shadows surrounding me faded, and the room grew lighter, as if the moon suddenly came out from behind the clouds and cast its rays into the barn. But that was impossible, because there was a thick fog that night. I had that strange feeling come over me again, like I was being watched.

Zebu kept his eyes fixed on the door behind me. I was afraid to look back, and hoped that the light would dim, and shadows return to the way they were a moment ago.

Zebu's eyes narrowed. He started to growl exactly the way he did back at the zoo when Miss Finch would step into his cage.

I looked back toward the door in shock, seeing Miss Finch holding a lantern, staring at me with wide stretched eyes and cheeks that flushed from pink to crimson red. She pointed at me with her mouth hanging wide open, shaking her fist. **"SO YOU'RE THE ONE WHO STOLE THE TIGER!** How could you do such a monstrous thing after I took such good care of you… and even shared my private house!"

I heard her breathing deepen, sounding as if she was out of breath. "You little thief! Do you have any idea how much trouble you got me into?"

She took three steps toward me, then stopped and stretched her mouth open again. "I was responsible for that tiger! You're no better than a common thief!"

She stomped toward me squinting. "You're going to pay for this!" she said, .

I backed away with my hands raised up in

107

front of me. That same moment, Zebu lunged between me and Miss Finch, blocking her way.

"Get out of my way, cat!" she snarled. "That is, if you know what's good for you!"

Zebu stood his ground, growling back, not showing any signs of fear. All his rage was focused on one person; the cruel zoo veterinarian who was standing right in front of him.

Miss Finch sneered at Zebu. "You don't even come close to scaring me." She kicked straw up into Zebu's face, just like she did so many times in the past. "Take that, cat!" she shouted, kicking more straw at him.

That must have been the last straw for Zebu, because he leaped forward and sunk his teeth into her leg. She somehow managed to stay on her feet and looked as if she was about to hit Zebu with the metal lantern, so I rushed forward and pushed her off balance onto the hay. Before she could get back up, Zebu leaped at her, knocking her flat on her back.

"Get off of me! Get off!" she shouted. Zebu kept her pinned down and repeatedly swiped his paw at her, starting from the base of her neck, going up to her forehead. She was no match against Zebu now. He had grown too powerful from eating all the extra steaks I gave him.

As much as Miss Finch disgusted me, I tried my best to pull Zebu off of her, but he was too strong and determined to have his revenge upon her.

She fought back like a wrestler, tossing, turning, trying her best to push him off, but quickly grew weaker and weaker with no hope of escape.

I raised my hands to the side of my head, feeling hopeless to stop the fight. I couldn't stand watch it a second longer, so I fled out of the barn.

CHAPTER 19

I ran down the road for about a mile, then stopped a moment and gazed back in the direction of the barn. I could still hear Miss Finch's faint cries in the distance. I hoped and prayed that Zebu didn't kill her, for if he did, I believed he would surely be hunted down and killed.

I thought that if the authorities caught me, I would be put behind bars for taking Zebu out of the zoo. Who would believe that I was trying to prevent a tiger from being starved to death, or from being sold to private game reserve to be hunted down and killed? How could I convince them when I couldn't even speak?

I gazed down the hill, and from out in the distance could see the ocean. I had a keen interest about the sea from what Higgins told me about it, and thought that it might offer me a place of refuge.

After traveling for about an hour, I finally reached the coastline. A gentle breeze blew in from the ocean and filled my lungs with the salty air. It felt so good to be free, and I was determined to do my best to keep it that way.

I peered over the edge of a high cliff and saw white-capped waves roll ashore, then crash and foam over slimy green rocks. I suddenly felt dizzy and backed away from the cliff.

Gazing southward, I spotted a lighthouse perched on the rocks, beaming its light out across the ocean.

To the north of me, from out in the distance, I was excited to see two sailing ships docked at a harbor.

After hiking along the coastline for about an hour, I finally reached the place where the ships anchored. A surge of excitement stirred within me as I gazed upon the sailing vessels. I pondered if perhaps one of them might become my ticket to a new life, in a new land, a wonderful place, where people might be of a kinder sort. I just had to figure out a way to get on one of those ships. I didn't have any money, and was unable to speak, so how could I do it? Without being able to talk, they might think I'm dumb, or maybe even crazy. I looked down at my clothes and new body, and thought, *at least I have a chance now, since I no longer look like the Mushroom Monster, and had on some decent clothes.* I knew that it would be difficult to find a way to get passage on one of those ships, and besides, I had no way of knowing where they would be going, but that was a risk I was willing to take.

CHAPTER 20

I saw crew hands on each ship mending nets, sharpening harpoons, and scrubbing the decks.

A fancy dressed man, but not too clean looking, walked about the ship's deck, inspecting the sailors' work. I heard someone call out his name. "Captain Graze," they said. He was a tall, young-looking fellow, except for his sunken cheeks and a peppered beard that draped across his thin chest. He had on a navy blue jacket with gold buttons running down the front. When he smiled I noticed that he was missing a few teeth on one side of his mouth, creating the impression of a dark hole leading inside. Strangely, the sight brought back nightmarish thoughts of the dark, gloomy cave where I was kept prisoner for so many years.

Captain Graze leaned against the side rail and shouted toward the ship docked across from his. "Captain Baker," he said. "Did you see any signs of Rage?"

Captain Baker crossed his arms in front of him. "No, Captain Graze, but I'm sure we'll be gettin' that devil whale soon." He turned and gave me a quick, unsavory stare, with squinty bloodshot eyes. Captain Baker had deep wrinkles spread across sun-baked copper skin, and was a stubby sort of man. A red bandana wrapped around his well-greased, coal-black hair, tied flat against the scalp, and a short ponytail hung on the nap of his neck.

I gasped when he turned sideways and saw the image of a blue whale with a harpoon pierced clear through its side tattooed on his left shoulder. The sight made my stomach churn.

Captain Baker faced the other ship. "Any news of the other two ships that went ah whaling to be gettin' Rage, Captain Graze?"

Captain Graze shook his head. "They be due back a month ago, they were. Perhaps that whale you be huntin' got 'em first. Biggest, meanest, of the Seven Seas, they say."

Captain Baker chuckled, "Stuff of fables, be it.

Need I be remindin' you, dear brother, the name of this here ship, "The Lucky Whaler?" We always be gettin' our whale."

Captain Graze sighed. "We lost one brother to that monster. Watch your stern. Can't afford to lose another."

"Aye, that be true. That be true." He reached into a wooden keg and pulled out a bone with a little bit of meat still left on it. A medium-sized, short hair brown dog, well muscled, with a broad head, stubby tail, and powerful looking jaws, licked his chops when he saw Captain Baker dangle the bone above his head.

"Hey, Brutus," said Captain Baker, with a smug grin. "How'd you like to addin' a nice juicy bone to your ribs?"

Brutus sat in front of him with his eyes sparkling at the bone. His jaw hung wide open, with the corners of his mouth raised, as if smiling, waiting to be tossed a tasty meal.

The dog repeatedly jumped up and down, trying to snatch the bone out of the captain's hand, but he kept raising it just out of his reach with each leap.

Instead of letting Brutus have it, the captain walked over to the side of the ship and dropped the bone into the water. Brutus ran over to the side of the ship, propped his front paws on the side railing, and sadly watched his bone sink into the murky water. He looked back at the captain and growled.

"Brother," said Captain Graze, grinning. "Brutus is goin' to be gettin' his revenge on you some day." He squinted at the dog's massive jaws. "Take you for a meal, perhaps, for teasing him. You best not always be teasing him too much. You got to be stopping that."

Captain Baker chuckled. "Aye, I'm just having ah little fun with him, I was." He looked down into Brutus's snarling face. "Time to time he need to be reminded who be the captain of this here ship."

I raised my hand to my chin and thought, *If I could be a stowaway on one of the two ships, I hoped it would be on Captain Graze's vessel.* It appeared to be newly painted, and even had a wooden mermaid attached to the bow, painted in blue and gold.

Captain Baker's ship, on the other hand, although it looked to be well built and seaworthy, had the appearance of being very old and weathered. I raised my nose and grimaced. The whole boat smelled of fish, and the odor made my stomach feel suddenly upset.

Attached to the bow of Captain Baker's ship

was a wood carving of a whale that looked as if it might be smiling. Head-to-tail, it must have been over six feet long and was painted blue.

I turned and saw three girls in their twenties, dressed in fancy blue, yellow, and pink dresses chatting on the dock next to Captain Graze's ship. Each lady had a special look about them. One had long, golden braided hair piled on top of her head. The second had very long, thick eyelashes, that didn't look real. The third lady had ruby red lips and a powdered white face. It appeared as if they were pointing and giggling at a poster. Even though I couldn't read that well, I was still curious about what it said, so I walked over to get a closer look. I ran my finger across each sentence, peering at each word close up. I wished that I could understand everything it said, but there were words written I was never taught the meaning of.

The lady with the golden hair stepped next to me. "Can't you read? The king of Nod, of the Kingdom of Bore, is having a singing contest." She smiled and raised her chin. "The maiden with the most beautiful voice in the all the land will win the hand of the king's son, Prince Arnold." She ran her eyes from my shoes up to the top of my head. "Too bad you're dressed like a pauper and all. Maybe if you could sing and afford a decent dress you could enter the contest too."

My head sank low in disappointment. As I started to walk away, the two other ladies stepped in front of me, blocking my way.

Now what do they want? I thought. Didn't I get enough insults for one day?

The lady with the red lips and powdered white face tapped me on the shoulder. "We have the best singing voices in all the land."

The lady with the long eyelashes moved closer and stared into my face. "No one has a chance to beat us. No one."

Such braggarts, I thought. When they giggled it sounded so lame. What arrogant, prideful women. I watched them huddle in a circle, giggle, glance my way, then suddenly walk up to me again.

The lady with the golden hair stood directly in front of me. "So strange you are. We never heard a peep out of you. Are you deaf?"

The lady with the ruby lips tilted her head at me and gave me a frown. "If only she could speak and sing, sister."

The lady with the golden hair swiped her hand at me. "Oh, don't even mention it to her. How could a deaf and mute girl win a princely hand?"

I was so happy to see the three bragging

women finally walk away and head up the boarding ramp onto Captain Graze's ship.

I didn't know what was worse now, spending days at sea with those three windbags on Captain Graze's ship, or having to stay on Captain Baker's smelly whaling boat.

Crew hands from each ship headed down the boarding ramp and made their way across the dock. They entered a red building, then moments later came out carrying crates and barrels to restock their ships.

I sneaked to the back of the storage building and was able to squeeze in between two loose boards to get inside. Next, I rolled a large empty barrel from the back wall to the front side door where they were loading supplies. I quickly climbed inside, then lowered the lid on top of my head. It was pitch dark inside. The walls smelled sweet and felt sticky to the touch, like molasses.

I could feel the barrel I was in suddenly tilt onto its side, then lift into the air. I couldn't help but wonder which ship I would be loaded onto.

CHAPTER 21

The barrel I was hiding in suddenly thumped to the floor. I heard men talking between themselves for a couple minutes. A moment later, it became very quiet, so I decided to take a chance and peep outside. Just as I was about to lift the lid, I heard someone start to snore. Not only snoring, but grunts and farts too. The sounds reminded me of Miss Finch. I couldn't forget how she snored, grunted, and let loose bursts of gas, which I hoped wasn't because of an upset stomach caused by my bad cooking. I figured that whoever was making those noises must be close by. I raised the lid a little and peeked out. *Oh my,* I thought. The mystery snorer was none other than the ship's dog, Brutus. I suddenly realized that I must be on "The Lucky Whaler," captained by the man with that dreadful looking tattoo of a harpooned whale on his shoulder.

I thought, this voyage is going to be one, big, nightmare.

I quickly lowered the lid, seeing Brutus suddenly open his eyes and sniff the air. I was told that dogs have a keen sense of smell, and was worried that he may have already picked up my scent.

A moment later, I heard sniffing and scratching sounds coming from just outside the barrel. I held my breath and thought, *Oh my gosh! He knows I'm in here. What am I going to do now?*

I waited until it became silent again, then took another look outside. I was surprised to see Brutus sitting three feet in front of me with what looked like a grin on his face, if that were possible, being that he's a dog.

I motioned with my hands for him to stay quiet and get away. Instead of barking, he jumped up against the side of the barrel and started rocking it back and forth.

I heard footsteps approaching, then a deep, raspy voice say, "What's be the matter with you, Brutus?"

Oh no!, I thought. It sounded just like Captain Baker!

Brutus jumped up against the side of the barrel and rocked me back and forth again. I tried to keep my balance, and prayed that the barrel wouldn't tip over, sending me sprawling out across the floor.

I heard the captain's voice again. "Brutus! Why ye be so interested in that barrel?" Brutus pawed and scratched the side of the container, whimpered, and made deep throated growls.

The footsteps grew louder and closer, then stopped. I took a deep breath and braced myself for the worst.

I heard the captain's voice again. "Brutus boy, you thinkin' food be in that barrel?"

I thought, *I'm done for now, and am sure to be found out.*

Sure enough, the lid lifted above my head. I looked up and saw Captain Baker's scowling face staring back down at me. He slowly moved his head side to side in a moment of silence, then raised one eye, squinting with the other. "Aye, what's we have here?" He grabbed my right shoulder and pulled me up. "A stowaway be ye. Get ye out from there."

My legs felt so cramped from having to squat in the same position for so long a time I could hardly stand up.

His face reddened. "Well... too far from shore

to makin' ah land lover out of you. You be earning your keep here, on this ship. You good at swabbing decks?"

I shook my head.

"Be ye good at… cookin' grub?"

I gave him a blank stare.

"Be ye deaf? Speak up, girl! Answer me! What be your name?"

I gestured with my hands to try and let him know I couldn't speak.

He cocked his head to one side, then raised his finger to his chin in a moment of reflection. "A mute, be thee? Well… you best be followin' my orders on this ship. A step in the wrong direction and over ye be goin', swimmin' with the sharks, be ye. Let's be prayin' you be takin' the right step forward… always."

He pointed his finger at me. "Share the load, work hard, and a passage to land you be gettin'. Understand?"

I quickly nodded.

The next thing I knew, I found myself on the ship's deck being introduced to the crew. I counted fifteen ship hands. There wasn't a clean-shaven man among them. Some had silver beads strung onto their braided beards.

The captain called over one of his sailors and

ordered him to get me something to clean the deck. He wasted no time in fetching a bucket of water and a flat stone.

Captain Baker pointed at the deck. "Scour ye well, then be expectin' a portion of food come evenin'."

I felt my stomach grumble from hunger and was all too eager to do any kind of chore to get some food. I got down on my hands and knees and slid the stone back and forth across the deck.

I looked to my left and saw a sailor scrubbing the deck on the other side of the ship. He started to laugh out loud. I thought, *Maybe he got crazy bored.* If I had to scour decks every day I think I might go crazy and start laughing my head off too.

The air felt hot and humid that day, with not even a whisper of breeze to cool the soul, or fill the sails. I worked hard, and after only a short time I could feel sweat bead on my forehead and roll down across my face. I had to constantly swipe the back of my hand across my forehead to keep the stinging sweat from getting into my eyes.

The captain was gracious enough to grant me a break after an hour's work. I walked over to the side of the ship and gazed out across an ocean that appeared to stretch endlessly. The air was perfectly still, and the ocean reminded me of a giant mirror, reflecting cloud and sky upon its surface.

I leaned against the side rail and took a deep breath of salty air. I was reluctant to gaze upon my reflection on the water's surface, or look into a mirror, for that matter, being fearful that I might once again see my previous mushroom face staring back at me. From time to time, I pinched myself just to make sure I wasn't dreaming and was still on this strange ship, voyaging across the open seas to a destination unknown. I kept dreaming of a brighter future, no matter how bleak the present may be.

A light breeze stirred the ocean's surface and the reflection of sky and clouds rippled away. I heard someone call out from behind. "Get back to work!" Whatever breaks we were allowed on ship, they weren't long enough.

A sudden gust of wind blew my hair back across my shoulders, and a sailor in the crow's nest high above me shouted, "Fair wind, at last, Captain."

I gazed upward and saw white sails flap in the breeze, then billow out firm.

Once again "The Lucky Whaler" was on its way, slicing through choppy waters. I was so excited to see a group of six large fish swimming alongside the ship. I wondered how they could possibly keep up with the boat for such a long time. They appeared to be so happy and carefree. I thought that they looked like such beautiful creatures. One of the crew hands said that they were called porpoises.

I closed my eyes and dreamed that we docked in a new land, where people treated others with love, compassion and kindness, if such a place ever exists, which I prayed it did. My dream was quickly interrupted by a firm tap on the back of my shoulder by one of the crew hands. The sailor introduced himself to me as Dizzy Dean. I thought that to be an unusual name, but when I saw his eyes start to roll around in his head, I understood how his name came to be.

Dizzy Dean stared at me with wide, wrinkled eyes. "Aye, Missy. Keep your eyes peeled for Rage." He stepped over to the side of the ship, glanced out across the ocean, then looked back at me again. "Rage be not any whale." He stretched his arms far apart. "The largest in the Seven Seas, said be he. Over sixty feet they say." He stepped closer and whispered into my ear. "A revenger for killing its mate, rumor say. A man-killer now, be he."

He stepped back, and stared at me with his skeleton-like body and sunken cheeks. "A destroyer of ships! Mighty head have he. Like steel! Crush the hulls, like a battering ram. Wood to splinters, come to pass." He looked over the side of the ship, then snapped his head back at me. "Men be taken to the deep, by Rage, never comin' back... never."

Dizzy jingled some coins in a brown leather pouch hanging from the side of his waist. "Aye, Rage be havin' a hefty bounty on him. Enough be for a new ship, perhaps. Keep them eyes peeled sharp, missy." He pointed toward a brass bell. "See that there, missy? Ring it loud, if ye be lucky, or perhaps unlucky enough to be gettin' first sight of Rage."

I nodded, but really didn't mean it. I didn't tell Dizzy, or rather couldn't, that I would never alert anyone to kill any animal, especially a magnificent creature such as a giant whale. Perhaps Rage wouldn't have become such a bad whale if his mate wasn't killed to fill oil lamps in some distant land. I would do everything in my power to prevent any harm to come to any whale, "Lucky Whaler" or not.

CHAPTER 22

Brutus had a bad habit of peeing on the ship's deck right after he finished eating. I saw the Captain and crew turn red-faced, shout unkind words, and even give chase to that poor dog for what he did. I was told that he could only go at one place on the boat, and that was in a special metal pan set aside just for him. Captain Baker would often hold back Brutus meals to punish him for not going in the right place. I didn't think it was Brutus's fault. Where else can a dog go to relieve himself on a ship besides a small pan without getting into trouble?

I blamed the cook, who loved to make all his dishes spicy-hot. He always tossed chopped red and green peppers into the cooking pot. My mouth felt like it was on fire right after eating his food. I always made sure I had a large glass of water next to me whenever I ate. I saw Brutus drink a lot of water right after he ate too.

As the days passed by, I noticed that Brutus was getting thinner and thinner. The conflict between Brutus and Captain Baker reminded me of how Miss Finch would punish and starve Zebu for not doing exactly what she wanted. I wasn't going to stand by and watch that dog go hungry, captain's orders or not.

******

I followed the cook from a distance one morning and discovered where he stored Brutus's food. Evening time, I made it a habit to sneak Brutus the meals he so deserved. For three weeks I was able to get him extra food. One evening I heard footsteps approaching and quickly hid Brutus's half-finished plate of food behind a wooden barrel.

My heart dropped when I saw Captain Baker round the corner. He stopped and stared at me suspiciously. I heard gobbling noises coming from behind the barrel, and so did the captain. When I looked back, I saw Brutus's stubby tail wagging like crazy from just behind the barrel. I thought, *Oh no! This is not good.*

Captain Baker's eyes narrowed. "Why suppose Brutus be appearin' so happy behind that keg?" He stepped behind the barrel. "Ah hah! What do we be havin' here?" he said, picking up Brutus's plate. "How ye be supposin' his dish be gettin' all the way over here?"

I was so relieved to see it empty and clean. *Good boy, Brutus. He ate up all the evidence.* But when I turned and looked down at Brutus's face, I cringed. He forgot to lick his chops, and had food stuck all around his mouth. I thought, *This is bad.*

The captain looked at me with red cheeks that I knew weren't from blushing. In a scary tone of voice I heard him say, "Caught you two scallywags red-handed, I did." He shook the plate in front of me. "Aye, sneaking my Brutus extra food, be ye?" He tossed the plate at my feet. "Now I know why Brutus be takin' a special likin' to you. I thought he be lookin' fat of late." He pointed his finger at himself. "I be the only one who be feedin' him," he said with a scowl. "How long ye be thinkin' you could keep this secret goin' behind me and crew?" He wrinkled his nose. "I be wondering why it be stinkin' over here of late."

I wished I could speak up and tell Captain Baker that he wasn't giving Brutus enough food to keep a frog from croaking. I thought, *You toad in a hole. Wart face.*

Captain Baker stepped closer. "If I be not such

a kindhearted soul, I'd be making you walk the plank this here second."

Right after Captain Baker said those words, Brutus walked up to him, raised his right leg, then released some yellow liquid onto his black boot. I was shocked when I saw him do that, but I believed the man deserved every ounce of it. Captain Baker gave Brutus a sharp kick with the side of his boot, sending him sliding against the side of the barrel. Next, he reached out and gripped my right shoulder. "To the jail with you," he said with a scowl.

On the way to the ship's prison I heard a voice shout down from the crow's nest.

"Rage! Starboard bow, Captain!"

Everyone stopped what they were doing and rushed over to the side of the ship.

I could hardly believe my eyes. There was Rage, big as life.

Crew hand Erik Myers leaned over the side rail and pointed. "Lookie there, Captain! Two harpoons logged squarely in his side!"

Another crew hand, Curley Banks, turned and spoke to the captain. "Be true, and each one painted the colors of the two missing ships."

I saw the harpoons in the whale's left side, one red, the other blue.

The air was still, and the ship lay dead in the water. Rage disappeared beneath the murky depths. All eyes focused on the ocean's surface, anxiously waiting for him to come up for air. Curley got his harpoon ready. One end of the coil of rope was tied to the spear, the other to the bow of the boat.

"What luck!" said the captain, spotting Rage rise from the deep and spout water close to port side. "Quick, land the spear. Make haste!"

Curley arched his harpoon back across his shoulder, then thrust it forward. It flew over the water and pierced Rage's left side, a foot away from the other spears.

Captain Baker grinned the instant the harpoon lanced the whale's side.

I grit my teeth and pressed my lips tightly together, worried about the whale's fate.

Rage swam dead ahead, and the rope quickly stretched taunt at the bow. Minutes later, the mighty whale tired from having to pull the ship forward.

Captain Baker grinned. "Soon he be weak as a newborn. Then he be ours for the takin'. Another trophy for... "The Lucky Whaler," he be."

After a few short minutes, Rage tired and couldn't pull the ship any further. He turned around, and appeared to be staring right back at us. The ship slowly glided forward. In a matter of seconds, the ship would be close enough to land another spear.

Eric readied his harpoon, preparing to seal the whale's fate. In just a moment it would be all over for Rage. I couldn't just stand by and watch that beautiful whale get slaughtered. I needed to take action and try to save that poor whale's life. I spotted a knife wedged between a sailor's pants and his black leather belt. I rushed up behind him, snatched the knife, and then sprinted to the bow of the boat. With every ounce of strength I had, I slashed the knife down upon the rope, slicing it clear through. It may have been my imagination, but it looked as if Rage was watching me the instant I cut the rope to set him free.

Two more harpoons were launched at Rage, but he had already put too much distance between himself and the ship. Captain Baker and the crew watched the harpoons fall short of their target and sink into the murky depths. Everyone slowly turned about, and looked me straight in the eye with what looked like a different kind of rage.

I dropped the knife to the deck and ran toward the stern until I could go no further. When I turned to look back, I was surprised to see Brutus standing between me and the angry mob. He growled and snapped his teeth at anyone who dared to get any closer to me. Captain Baker stepped up to Brutus and kicked him aside with his boot, sending him sliding across the deck and up against the side rail. He stared at me with bloodshot eyes. "You be deservin' twenty lashings, then to be a tasty meal for the sharks... but that be too quick a punishment. Take her away." Two crew hands promptly dragged me off to jail, then locked me behind bars. I was thankful that I wasn't lashed, and then thrown to the sharks.

What a brave dog Brutus was, to stand up against Captain Baker and the entire crew like that. A minute later, I saw Brutus limp inside my jail room, then sit in front of my cell, looking as if he was actually worried about me. I reached through the bars and ran the palm of my hand back across his head. I saw tears swell in the corners of his eyes, then bead down the sides of his snout. Was it possible that a dog could have such love and compassion for me, as I have for him?

Just when I felt like there was no hope for me to escape from this prison, I remembered what the angel once said to me when I was back in the cave; "When your pain becomes so great you think you cannot bear it, you will have unspeakable joy, if you endure the trials, keep the faith, and live a life in love and kindness for others." I did have a moment of joy when I saw my new face and body. However, now I was in another jail, cave of sort, with the promise of a better life rusting away like the iron bars before me. I had learned much patience and endured great pain already through the many years I suffered as the Mushroom Monster. I started to think of a plan of escape for me and Brutus. My eyes were drawn to the keys hanging on a wooden peg on the other side of the room.

CHAPTER 23

I was surprised to see Dizzy Dean step into my jail room right after dark holding a lantern in one hand, and a plate of food in the other. One side of his face was shadowed, giving him an extra spooky look, especially with his large white eyes rolling around in his head for what seemed like forever.

Dizzy knelt down and slid the plate of food across the floor into my cell. "Here... this spicy meal be for you."

I gestured with my hands that I appreciated the food, and started to take bites of it as he continued to talk.

"I'd be admirin' ye bravery out there today, but your life now be in peril for sure." He leaned forward, raised his hand, and curled his finger for me to move closer. He put his face up against the bars and stared at me with squinty eyes. "Want to be hearin' ah secret?" he said with a grin.

I took a deep breath and nodded, but really wasn't sure if I wanted to hear any of Dizzy's secrets or not.

He looked over his shoulder toward the door a moment, then back at me. "They think I be crazy, they do." He pointed at me, then laughed like he really was crazy. "Tell yah another secret. I don't enjoy killin' whales neither." He stared at me through the bars with wide rolling eyes. "The Lucky Whaler be not so lucky now. Dead in water, she be. There be no breeze takin' us to escape the wrath to come." He started to laugh crazy again, and I took two steps back away from the bars.

He grinned, and then continued to say, "Rage be circling about. Yes, around, and round, and round he go! Where he be comin' about, nobody knows." He pointed at me, then at himself. "Like we be the prey, and he be... well... the hunter." He curled his finger for me to move closer, but I stood my ground, not certain if he really was crazy or not. He looked back at the door, then back at me. "I be telling them before, not to be huntin' Rage, but they don't listen. Think me to be crazy, they do. Do you be believin' I'm crazy?"

I shook my head.

Dizzy stared at me dead on, then gave me a spooky grin. "The Lucky Whaler be thick-hulled for a time as now," he whispered. "The time be comin' to test it soon." He stepped toward the door, then stopped and looked back at me with his rolling eyes. "Watch ye. Time be comin' soon. Watch ye." With those parting words, he disappeared out of the room.

I think he was telling me to get ready for something bad, but even if that was the case, there was little I could do, being trapped behind these bars and all. How was I was going to escape? My fate seemed so uncertain now after spoiling Captain Baker's prize kill. I was also worried about Brutus, and the possibility that the captain might try to starve him for something that wasn't his fault.

******

I awakened early the next morning just in time to see the first rays of the breaking dawn cast beams of light out across the floor before me. That same instant, I felt a sudden crash against the side of the ship so powerful it knocked me clear out of bed. My head hit the floor. Everything around me became a blur. I leaned up and shook my head, trying to clear my mind. I heard the captain and crew shouting outside, and the sound of footsteps running to and fro.

"Rage be comin' about," one of the sailors shouted.

Minutes later, I felt another crash against the hull, this time coming from the opposite side of the ship so strong it knocked me off my feet. The next thing I knew, the boat started to lean to one side. An eerie silence followed, but it didn't last for long. Another sailor shouted, "The ship be takin' on water, Captain!"

I was startled to see Dizzy Dean suddenly appear at the entranceway. He laughed like crazy, then fell silent a moment before saying, "Tide be turnin' against 'The Lucky Whaler.' Down she be. Down she goes." After saying those words of doom, he suddenly vanished.

I had a hard time understanding everything Dizzy said to me, but those words rang true. It seemed to me that "The Lucky Whaler's" luck has just run out.

I felt another blow against the side of the ship more powerful than the last. Captain Baker shouted out for a damage report, but no one answered. I gazed down at the deck beneath my feet and heard what sounded like water gushing through the hull.

Another voice rang out that sounded like Curley. "Sinking she be, Captain!"

I heard Captain Baker shout back, "Abandon ship! Let loose the rowboats!"

My heart sank low when I heard the captain shout those orders. I hoped to see someone rush inside to take me with them, but no one came for me or Brutus, who stayed faithfully by my cell.

They couldn't be so cruel to let us go down with the ship, could they? They probably blamed me for what happened, and I guess they had the right to think so. A couple minutes passed and no one came.

The sounds of water gushing through the hull grew louder, and I felt the boat start to keel more to one side.

Just when I thought things couldn't get any worse, the ship was struck again, but this time it turned out to a blessing in disguise, because the jail keys got knocked off the wooden peg and dropped onto the floor. I motioned for Brutus to fetch the keys over and over again, but he just stood there, looking confused as what to do.

The ship continued to tilt, and the keys started

to slide across the floor, stopping not far from my cell. I stretched my hand out through the bars to grab them, but the tips of my fingers came up a few inches short. I quickly removed my shoe and reached out through the bars a second time while holding the shoe out in front of me. I was able to slide the keys back just enough to grab hold of them.

My hand felt so shaky, I could barely hold the key steady enough to slide it into the lock. I hurried out of the jail and onto the ship's deck with Brutus right by my side.

I spotted Captain Baker, Curly, Dizzy Dean and the rest of the crew in two small boats about a quarter mile out from the ship.

Rage rose from the deep directly in front of their boats, blocking their way of escape. Next, he started to swim in circles around them. The crew stopped rowing, and I could see their heads rolling around and around, following Rage's every move.

After circling three times, Rage swam up to the rowboats, then raised his monstrous tail above the crew. I saw Captain Baker and another sailor dive overboard just moments before the tail slammed down. The small boats shattered to pieces. Splinters of wood flew into the air in every direction. It was a horrible sight to behold.

I saw Captain Baker and one other sailor, I think it was Dizzy Dean, surface twenty feet away from the wreckage. Rage swam up to Captain Baker and Dizzy, then pushed them forward through the water with the front of his head toward what was left of "The Lucky Whaler" until they were pressed between the ship's hull and his head. I heard two brief screams, then saw tentacles of red bleed through the water.

CHAPTER 24

The Lucky Whaler was taking on water fast, and I knew it would be just a matter of minutes before the ship would sink. I had no other choice, but to take my chances on the open sea. When I looked over the side rail, my eyes stretched wide with hope spotting a fifteen-foot piece of the ship floating on the water directly below me. Painted onto its side was the name of the ship, "The Lucky Whaler."

I didn't know how to swim. Brutus's safety was my first concern. I tried my best to coax him to jump overboard first, but he refused to go without me. I couldn't take a chance on jumping first, not knowing for sure if he would follow, so after a short prayer, I jumped off the ship with Brutus securely in my arms.

I felt dizzy and lightheaded as I descended into the water. I hoped to land close enough to grab hold of the edge of the raft as I hit the water, but that was not to be, and instead I felt my body submerge several feet beneath the water's surface. I looked up through the murkiness and saw Brutus paddling upward with tiny bubbles rising all around him. That same moment, I felt my body slowly sinking deeper, with no way to make it back to the surface.

Just when I thought all hope was lost, a miracle happened. I felt Brutus's body brush against my right shoulder. He must have swam back to try to rescue me. I reached up and was able to grab hold of his collar. He thrashed and kicked like crazy to get us back up to the surface. Moments later, I was able to reach up and grab hold of the edge of the raft. The instant my head broke the water's surface I gasped for air, filling my lungs with sweet oxygen.

Brutus was so exhausted and weak from trying to rescue me, he didn't have any fight left in him, and started to sink beneath the water. With one hand holding onto the edge of the raft, I submerged my body, and stretched my other arm down toward Brutus. My heart skipped a beat when I felt my hand grab onto his collar. I quickly pulled his head back above the water's surface. He didn't move. With much struggle, I was able to slide him up onto the floating piece of wreckage.

I kneeled beside his motionless body and started to pump his chest. I took a deep sigh of relief when I saw his eyes open. He had not even an ounce of strength left to turn his head. I reached down, cradled him in my arms, and held his head snugly against my cheek.

I only had a brief moment of peace before Rage, that terror of the deep, rose to the surface. He headed right for us, about a quarter mile out. As he got closer, I could plainly see the three harpoons logged in his side, each one a different color, representing the ships he sank, the last one being, "The Lucky Whaler."

That mighty monster headed toward us like a battering ram. I thought, *This is the end,* and we would suffer the same fate as Captain Baker, Dizzy Dean, and the rest of the crew. I hugged Brutus and gave him one last kiss on the side of his snout. I thought he was the best dog I ever had, but then, he was the only dog I ever knew and loved. He meant so much to me.

I prayed to God that by some miracle we might be spared. When Rage got within about a hundred feet from us, I braced myself and closed my eyes, expecting at any moment to feel his crushing blow, and be knocked off the raft, back into the murky water. Seconds later, which seemed like an eternity, my eyes sprung open. I was amazed not to see Rage anywhere. Where did he go? It was as if he vanished into thin air. I leaned to one side and peered over the edge of the raft. His monstrous shadow passed directly beneath us. That same moment, I felt our raft suddenly swish back several feet toward the shadow.

Rage rose from the deep and headed for us a second time. I wondered if he was just playing games with us before deciding to crush us with his massive head or tail.

I slid my palm over Brutus's eyes and made another prayer before squeezing my eyes shut. A minute later, I was surprised that nothing happened again. I slowly opened my eyes and was shocked to see Rage floating perfectly still just a few feet away from us.

His giant eye exchanged glances between me and Brutus. We stared at each other for several minutes. It was very quiet that moment, without even the slightest whisper of breeze. All I could hear was the faint sound of water lapping against the side of the raft.

I didn't know how to explain it, but I didn't feel frightened anymore. As a matter of fact, I actually felt like I was in the company of two friends who

146

thought kindly of me for trying to help them in their time of need.

Could Rage's gentle nature toward me be because he saw me cut the rope, and set him free? Whales looked like they have a lot of room in their head for a big brain to figure things out.

Rage floated closer, then exchanged glances between me and the end of the rope that was attached to the harpoon. I felt as if he wanted me to grab hold of it. Being stranded out in the middle of the ocean offered little hope for survival, so I decided to take a chance and grasped the end of the rope in my hand. To my surprise, Rage started to pull our raft forward, and out across the open sea.

Several hours later, my hands cramped from having to hold onto the rope for such a long time. I spied a large nail sticking half way out of the side of the raft, and was able to secure the end of the rope to it. I looked down at Brutus and took note that he still appeared to be very weak and exhausted. I bet he was worried, just like me, about being stuck on a raft in the middle of the ocean, being pulled ahead by a giant whale to who knows where.

My eyes drifted open and shut until I finally fell asleep. Hours later, I awakened to a full moon spreading a glittering pathway of light out across the ocean's surface, with Rage pulling us right up through the middle of it.

I gazed up into the night sky and beheld another sea of sparkling lights, not of water, but a heavenly realm where I discovered, not long ago, that dreams can, and really do come true.

******

I had no idea where Rage was taking us, or if he had any intention of bringing us to land. I laid down with Brutus resting by my side for a time before falling asleep.

When I awakened the next morning, I discovered that we were in the midst of a thick fog. I squinted out in front of me, but was unable to see more than a few feet ahead, not even enough to see Rage's tail. The only way I knew he was still there was the constant forward motion of our raft.

A couple hours later, I heard what sounded like seagulls flying overhead. *There must be land nearby, I thought.* The sun burned off the haze, and my pulse quickened, seeing land come into view. Rage pulled us as close to shore as he dare. I reached over the side of the raft and ran the palm of my hand in soft circles upon the side of Rage's head as my way of telling him how thankful we were for sparing our lives and bringing us safely to land.

Brutus exchanged glances between the whale and the shore. I somehow felt that he too was thankful for what that great creature of the deep did for us.

Rage floated closer to the raft, and I was able to untie the rope attached to the harpoon. I dearly wanted to remove the spears from his side, but the barbed ends, I believed, would make it impossible to do it without causing him too much pain.

Rage moved away from the raft and headed back to open water. I took a deep breath, smiled, and waved goodbye to that great creature of the deep. He dove under the water a moment, then rose again, spouting a stream of water high into the air. I wondered if that was his way of saying goodbye. I kept my eyes fixed on that great whale until he disappeared back into the ocean depths from whence he came. I'll never forget that wonderful whale as long as I live.

CHAPTER 25

I was able to remove a strip of wood from the raft and use it as a paddle to get to shore. I felt so happy to finally make it back to land and step onto solid ground. The first thing I did was to wrap my arms around Brutus and give him a big hug and kiss.

I approached three buildings by the water's edge constructed of wood planks deeply cracked and splintered. One structure was built on stilts, with half the building perched out over the shoreline.

Brutus stayed right by my side as I headed around to the front of one of the buildings. There was a large sign hanging above the door that said, "The Salty Cracker." It looked like it might be a good place to try and get something to eat for me and Brutus. I hoped and prayed the people inside would be friendly. I was eager to do any kind of work to get some food, even if it meant cleaning tables, if that's all they had for me to do.

The minute I walked through the spring-hinged doors I spotted someone who looked to be the exact image of Captain Graze. He suddenly looked back over his shoulder at me. He had sunken cheeks and a mangy peppered beard. His piercing stare made the hairs on my arm stand on end. The corners of his mouth started to rise and form a big smile. Yep, that was Captain Graze all right. He had the same missing teeth I remembered seeing him have back at the dock where I first set sail.

The instant he saw Brutus, his smile dropped from his face. He quickly got up from his chair and pointed at him. "That dog lookin' to be like my brother's Brutus," he said, stepping closer with narrowed eyes. "Aye... that sure be him." He glared at me, and raised his voice. "My brother always be takin' Brutus where's he be goin'." He flashed his arm straight out, pointing at me. "How come he be with you?"

I stepped back and tried to let him know that I couldn't speak.

"A mute, be ye?" He stepped over to the window and stared out. I bet he was expecting to see his brother's ship anchored somewhere nearby. I suddenly became very worried. *I sure hope he didn't see our raft with the words to his brother's ship on it, "The Lucky Whaler."* How could I explain what happened to his brother, crew, and ship... not being able to speak? Besides, how could be believe the story of how a giant blue whale sunk his brother's ship, killed the crew, spared our lives, and then pulled us on a raft safely back to land? I crossed my fingers, hoping he would step away from the window before he saw the raft.

I needed to distract him away from the window, so I walked over to his table and made it look like I accidently knocked his drink onto the floor. That got his attention in a hurry. He snapped his head toward me and said, "Clumsy woman! Stand clear of the table."

The waiter rushed over, cleaned up the mess, then put a fresh drink on his table. He whispered into my ear, "Better be more careful. The Captain be not too forgivin' a man."

Captain Graze stepped away from the window, and I took a deep sigh of relief, thinking that he didn't see our raft. Just as I was beginning to feel a little more relaxed, he quickly turned back and looked out through the window a second time. I heard his breathing deepen and saw his eyes narrow. *I wondered if he spotted our raft with the name of his brother's ship.*

He moved his face up against the window, almost to the point of pressing his nose against the glass. "No! No!" he shouted. "Can't be true!"

I thought, *Oh no!* I was certain he'd seen the raft now.

He grumbled and muttered words I never heard before, and wished I never would again.

He stepped up to me and put his face close to mine. I got a whiff of his breath and stretched my head back. I thought that it smelled worse than a sewer.

He raised his finger and poked my shoulder. "What happen to me brother's ship and crew?"

I shook my head.

He leaned closer, raising his voice. "A second time… I be demandin', where be my brother, crew and ship!"

I shook my head again, unable to answer. He already knew that I was mute. How did he expect me to answer him? I grimaced, feeling his hand grip my shoulder. That same instant, Brutus ran up to Captain Graze's side, growling and snapping his teeth. The captain let me loose, took three steps back, then placed the palms of his hands out in front of him. "Easy now there, Brutus," he said, casting a slight grin.

Long strands of salvia oozed out the corners of Brutus's mouth onto the floor.

The captain gave me a nasty look. "What kind of spell ye be puttin' on that dog, you being a stranger and all?"

When Captain Graze shook his fist at me, Brutus growled and snapped his teeth the more.

I turned and ran out the front door. I glanced back over my shoulder and saw Captain Graze race down the front steps and take chase after me. I sprinted as fast as my legs could carry me to widen the gap between us.

"I'd be not through with you yet!" he shouted. "Get ye back!"

I glanced back and saw Brutus leap toward the captain, biting his leg from behind. He tripped and slid across the gravel road.

"Get back!" he shouted, leaning up with a bloodied cheek. "I be not through with you!" he continued to rant.

I ran down the road a ways, then veered off into the forest. I stopped for a moment, then clapped my hands three times, hoping that Brutus would hear me and come running back, but he never did. I wished I had a voice to call out to him.

I fled deeper into the forest. Every few minutes I looked back over my shoulder, hoping to see my friend Brutus. I prayed for his safety and wondered if I would ever see my dear friend again.

CHAPTER 26

The deeper I fled into the forest, the more fearful I became of what hidden dangers may lay just ahead of me. After about an hour's journey, I was fortunate to find some patches of wild berries. I was so hungry, that in no time at all, I stripped the prickly bushes of their fruits and filled my belly. I gazed down at my shirt and saw red and blue stains. *Oh well,* I thought, *at least it's not rotten food stuck to my shirt, like I had to endure in the past as the Mushroom Monster.*

I traveled along a narrow trail that snaked its way through a dense grove of pines. The path looked to be manmade, but not used in quite a while, with stretches of it overgrown with bushes and wild grass. I followed the trail for about another mile until I reached the edge of a large clearing. My eyes stretched wide with excitement spotting a log cabin at the far end of the meadow. *I wondered if anyone was home, and if they would take kindly to strangers, or perhaps try to chase me off.*

As I neared the cabin, I could see that the front door was part way open. I wanted to call out to see if anyone was home, but couldn't. I walked across the front deck, then reached out and rapped my knuckles upon the door, but no one answered. The only sounds I could hear were the honeybees collecting pollen from fields of blue, yellow, and pink wildflowers that spread as a thick blanket across the meadow around me.

I leaned up on my toes and peeped in through the side window. It appeared to be barren inside, with the exception of a table, two chairs, and a bed that leaned sideways, having one broken leg. All the furniture appeared to have been made from the nearby pine trees. I walked to the other side of the cabin and peered in through the other window. There were a half dozen canned goods scattered across the kitchen floor. The berries I had earlier that day didn't do much to keep my hunger down, and the sight of solid food made my stomach start to grumble.

The sun dipped below the horizon, and the pine trees spread fingers of shadow across the meadow. I took twenty paces away from the cabin and peered out in every direction. I was fearful of what wild creatures might be lurking about in the forest at night, and decided it best take my chances inside the cabin until morning. My main worry was that the owners might suddenly return home and catch me in their cabin while I lay asleep, but that was a chance I had to take.

The instant I entered the cabin I saw animal footprints left on the dusty floor. I leaned forward to get a closer look and noticed that most of the paw prints appeared to head toward the bed, and then back out the door.

I figured the animal that left those tracks must have been huge. I laid the palm of my hand on top of one of the prints and spread my fingers apart. It appeared to be, perhaps, as much as seven inches across. Just the thought of coming face-to-face with that animal sent shivers up my spine. I was beginning to have second thoughts about staying overnight in the cabin, but had nowhere else to go for shelter.

I stepped out onto the front porch and clapped my hands several times in hopes that

Brutus would hear me and come running across the meadow, but sadly, he was nowhere in sight. My shoulders slumped low, and I sighed in disappointment.

I stepped into the kitchen and stared at the canned food spread across the floor. My stomach reminded me that it was time for my next meal. I found a small knife in one of the kitchen drawers and used it to poke an opening in one of the cans. I discovered that it was filled with beans. I ate what was inside one, plus two other cans. They sure gave me a lot of gas. I wondered if Brutus was here now if he'd prefer to sleep outside in the fresh air.

The last rays of sunshine dipped below the horizon, and darkness fell upon the land. I lit an oil lamp left on the kitchen table, then walked over to the side window and looked out. From way out in the distance, toward the mountaintop, I saw the silhouette of a wolf with his head raised high, howling against a full moon. The only other sounds I could hear were the crickets chirping and frogs croaking.

I walked over to the bed and noticed that in addition to having one broken leg, the other three support posts were bent, and all leaned to one side. I thought that either someone did a lot of bouncing on the bed, like some kids, or some creature, that must have weighed a ton, had been sleeping on it. I hoped that it wasn't the latter, and prayed that I didn't encounter any scary beasts while staying overnight in the cabin.

I laid on the bed with my eyes closed for about an hour, but couldn't get to sleep. All of a sudden, my eyes snapped open, not from what I heard, but from what I didn't hear. The crickets and frogs fell silent and I couldn't help but wonder if some creature might be lurking about outside. I walked over to the window and peered out through the moon lit shadows, but couldn't see anything unusual. A moment later, I felt more relaxed as the crickets and frogs once again resumed their music.

I went back to bed and closed my eyes. A couple minutes later, the crickets and frogs fell silent again. I sat up in bed and listened for anything unusual. All of a sudden, I heard sniffing and scratching sounds coming from just outside the front door. *Brutus! Yes, it must be Brutus!* I rushed over and flung the door wide open, expecting to see my dear friend leap into my arms, but instead saw something that horrified me. I found myself face-to-face with a large bear that must have stood five feet tall at the shoulders.

The beast locked eyes with me, then leaned

up on his hind legs and let loose a ferocious roar. I slammed the door shut in front of him, locked it, then rushed over to the side window and looked out, but couldn't see the bear anywhere. I thought, *Where did he go?*

The bear's face suddenly flashed into view on the opposite side of the window as I was looking out. He roared, staring back at me with wide, glowing eyes. I stumbled to the floor and backed away from the window, tripping on the bed behind me. When the bear saw me on the bed his eyes stretched even the wider, like he was crazy mad about something. He growled and showed his teeth, swaying his head side to side in wide sweeping motions.

He disappeared from view, then a moment later, I heard him pounding and crashing against the front door, over and over again. Each time his massive body hit the door I could feel the entire cabin shake. A mist of fine dust dropped down from between the ceiling posts. I raised my hand to my mouth and started to cough.

Something suddenly caught my attention on the bed cover. It was a clump of brown matted fur, the same as the bear's. Even the color and length looked to be the same. There was no doubt in my mind that it belonged to that hairy monster outside. *He was probably using the cabin to sleep in at night, and I was in his private bed!* That explained all the paw prints leading to the bed and back out the door.

I clasped my hands together and prayed to be delivered from this monster. How could I survive a face to face encounter with a monster beast like that?

The bear took turns staring at me through the window, then kept going back to the front door to try and break it down.

My whole body quaked and trembled every time I heard him crash against the door. I felt my heart pounding in my chest. I shook my head, squeezed my eyes shut, and prayed that he would just stop and go away. I looked around me and thought, *I'm trapped with no way to escape! It's too late to get out!*

Finally, for what seemed like forever, but in reality was only a few short minutes, the unthinkable happened. The bear rammed against the door so hard it ripped away from the wood frame and came crashing down onto the cabin floor in front of me. The bear wasted no time and charged inside, trampling over the door as he went. My eyes bulged wide as I tried to scream, but couldn't. The bear leaned up on his hind legs in front of me, appearing so tall, I thought his head might hit the ceiling. He raised his paw with its dagger like claws at me, looking as if he was going to swipe me across the side of the head. I flashed my arms up in front of my face. The fear was too great, I felt like I couldn't stand the horror a second longer. That moment, when I thought all hope was lost, another miracle happened in my life. The bear raised his paws to the side of his head, looking as if he was trying to cover his ears, then backed away. I looked around me, hearing the windows hum and vibrate, but it wasn't caused by the bear's roar, it was me. I had found my voice!

I took another breath and screamed so loud, in such a high pitch, that one of the windows shattered. The bear turned and ran! I felt this queer sense of instant power and did something really crazy. I jumped up from the bed and chased that hairy monster clear out of the cabin and across the open field. Every time the bear stopped to look back, I screamed again, and he took off running like a scared rabbit until he finally disappeared into the forest.

I thought, *This must be a dream! My wild imagination! This can't be happening.* I heard myself laugh for the first time in my life. I thought I sounded like the crazy laughing sailor, Dizzy Dean on the not so "Lucky Whaler." Did I really find my voice? I pinched my arm just to make sure I wasn't dreaming, then made another high-pitch sound. *Yes! Yes! This is for real. It really must be true.* I felt so excited I hopped up and down in a circle like some kind of crazy rabbit saying, "Yes, yes, yes!"

******

I stepped out onto the front porch the next morning, spread my arms apart, and gazed out across the fields of flowers. Next, I sang several sweet songs Higgins taught me, which I memorized from heart. It was an amazing experience, so wonderful I could hardly imagine it.

My heart seemed to flutter like the butterflies that circled about. A minute later, rabbits, squirrels, and even the deer suddenly appeared out from the edge of the forest and stared back at me. They didn't seem to be afraid, but instead moved closer, as if they really liked my singing. What a beautiful gift from God, not only to be able to speak, but also sing with such a voice that even His creatures, like the rabbit and the deer came to hear me sing.

CHAPTER 27

Oh my, what shall I have for breakfast this morning? I thought. There were three cans of beans left sitting on the kitchen table. I must say, they made my first cabin experience a real gas. I didn't know how long it might be before I could find more food, so I forced myself to eat every last bean. After my boring, but hearty meal, I figured it was time to continue on with my journey and see where fate would lead me next.

I hiked back down the same path that I came until I reached the main road. Gazing southward, I could see "The Salty Cracker." I stepped to the middle of the road and called out for Brutus, but he was nowhere in sight. I realized that he never heard my voice before, so I would seem like a stranger calling out to him.

I decided to head north, and stay on the main road to see where it might lead me. I strode as fast as I could up a steep hill, anxious to see what may be on the other side. When I reached the top, my eyes stretched wide with excitement, seeing a town out in the distance.

About thirty minutes later, I arrived at the edge of the town center. I saw people dressed in fancy clothes stroll up and down the streets. Others rode in horse-drawn carriages. Everyone seemed to stare, point, and frown at me as they passed by. I suppose my berry-stained shirt made quite a fashion statement, but in a negative sort of way. I knew that I looked out of place, but what could I do? What I had on was all that I owned.

I saw a man drive by in his carriage with a large dog sitting beside him. The man and the dog had fluffy white hair so thick and long it nearly covered their eyes. They were both dressed in a white shirt, red bow tie, and black top hat. Higgins said that some people look like their dogs, but in this case, I think the dog looked more like the owner.

I thought the town to be a fascinating place to go exploring, with its many shops, selling a wide variety of items. I walked down the sidewalk, past red brick storefronts adorned with hanging wall baskets planted with red, pink, and white petunias.

The window displays were framed with green, squared off posts. Painted above the storefronts, in large bold letters, were the names of their businesses. The Old Bore Tea Shop, Royal Crown Books, Bentley Clothes, and Dover Antiques, were the names of just a few of them. They were all filled with beautiful and interesting gift and foods items.

The Red Cavalier Restaurant had several tables set out front with red umbrellas to help keep their customers cool and shaded. One of my favorite stores was Newman's Toy Shop, with its shiny red door. I peered in through the front window and saw something that immediately caught my attention; three stuffed bears all sitting in a row, dressed in orange, green, and yellow knit sweaters.

I headed across the street and approached a business called "The Gallant Knight." They had many beautiful landscape paintings for sale inside. I thought of Higgins's artwork, and how some of it, in my opinion, appeared to be even better than the ones on display. I wished that he could get discovered so he could sell his work there. It was such a beautiful store. It even had miniature gardens and small pools of water with colorful fish swimming about in each. Hanging on either side of the front door were two wire cages, each containing a parrot having green, red and yellow feathers. I watched the shoppers stroll around, admiring the paintings. Every minute or two, I heard one the parrots squawk by the front door and say, "Welcome! Welcome!" I was amazed how the birds could speak like that.

I started to get a little bored, so I headed around the corner and discovered an interesting store called "Hackey's Hat Shop." When I peered in through the front window I was shocked to see the same three ladies that boarded Captain Graze's ship before I stowed away on the whaling ship. As much as I disliked them, I thought that they may be the only ones who could offer me some kind of help.

The moment they stepped out onto the sidewalk, they started to argue amongst themselves about whose hat looked the prettiest. One of them looked back at me, then raised her finger to her chin, looking as if she was trying to think of something. A smile suddenly sprouted on her face. "Yes, now I remember," she said. "Aren't you the one who lost her voice, where we first set sail?"

"Yes, and I can speak now. I'm in need of a job for food and lodging. Can you help me?"

The three ladies walked in a tight circle around me, staring at my clothes, pouting, and shaking their heads. The next moment, they stepped several feet away from me, then huddled and whispered amongst themselves, as if in some kind of secret meeting. A minute later, they turned and faced me. The one with the golden hair braided on top of her head spoke up. "Would you consider... being our maid servant?"

I really didn't like the idea of having to be their servant, but felt I didn't have anywhere else to go for food and shelter, and besides, I was very hungry. I agreed to their offer, and felt as if I was already an experienced maid after having to slave hand and foot for Miss Finch in the past.

They formally introduced themselves to me. The girl with the golden hair braided on top of her head said her name was Gilda. The one with the long fake eyelashes said her name was Beatrice. And lastly, the girl with the ruby red lips and powdered white face introduced her herself to me as Paula. They stacked boxes of clothes in my arms so high I could barely see where I was going.

Gilda gazed back over her shoulder and waved me forward. "Hurry now! Don't dilly dally.

We haven't got all day."

A minute later, Beatrice stopped and stared back at me with her hands pressed firmly on her hips. "Oh my gosh, you are a slow one. Come on. Hurry up. Hurry up. I hope you can clean our house faster that you can walk."

Paula grinned. "Get those legs moving, maid! We simply must get back soon and practice our singing for the princely contest." She waved me forward with both hands. "No time to waste now, hurry up."

I felt faint and dizzy from having to walk for several hours already that day to get from the cabin to town, and really didn't appreciate their pushy behavior. I was worried, that at any moment, my legs would give out and I would stumble forward, casting their boxes filled with fancy clothes out across the sidewalk.

CHAPTER 28

I was so relieved when we finally reached the sisters' house and had their heavy boxes unloaded from my arms.

Gilda shook her head and pointed at me. "You're much too filthy to step foot in our house. Just how did you manage to get so many stains on those clothes?"

I kept silent, afraid that if I told her the whole story leading up to how I got to this land they might have me fired, or hand me over to the authorities to be questioned about the disappearance of "The Un-Lucky Whaler."

After having to wait for some time on their front steps, Beatrice finally waved me inside, then led me to a back room that had a large wooden tub filled with water. "Servant, go in there and take a bath while I see if I can find some suitable maid's clothes."

Paula nodded. "Yes, maid's clothes would

definitely be an improvement over those filthy stained rages. Yes, indeed."

A short time later Gilda handed me a plain white maid's dress, baker's hat, and an odd looking pair of green shoes that were squared off at the front.

"Be careful to not soil the lovely maid's clothes we most graciously let you borrow," said Gilda.

While making a change of clothes, I overheard Beatrice talking to her sisters in the next room. "Really now," she said. "I don't know how we came to be so generous to hire such a maid as that. I don't know what got into us. I really don't."

I looked out the window and saw black clouds billowing in from the East. Thunder rumbled in the distance, followed by flashes of lightning. A minute later, it started pouring rain.

I walked across the kitchen floor, through the hallway, and into the living room. There they were, the three lovely sisters with the extra wide shoes and mouths. They reminded me of three plump hens taking turns at cackling, "la, lah, la, lah, la, lah, lah, lah."

I got a sudden earache and rushed back into the kitchen. Fortunately, I was able to find a cotton ball. I pulled it in half, dampened it with water, then stuffed each ear. Ah, it felt so nice to have a moment of quietness. How they thought they were going to win any singing contest was beyond me.

When I entered the living room I saw Gilda point at me with her mouth flapping about. Then I realized she was calling out for me to get her something, so I reached up and removed one of the pieces of cotton from my ear.

"Maid, what's wrong with you?" said Gilda, getting up from the sofa. She sneered at me. "Really, can't you hear? What did you take out of your ear?"

I chuckled. "Just some cotton to help with a sudden earache. That's all. I don't normally have earaches."

Paula waved her hand at me. "What kind of servant are you? Hurry up now. Get us some tea. Pull yourself together, or we'll be compelled to send you back out into the street."

I was surprised to hear a knock on the front door when it was raining so hard outside. All three sisters looked my way and gave me dirty look. "Well, hurry up now," said Gilda. "Go see who it is!"

When I opened the door, I saw an elderly man standing outside, soaking wet. He reached out and handed me a nicely wrapped package with a pretty gold ribbon on top. Beatrice rushed over and snatched the box out of my hand. "That's "*my*" pearl necklace!" she said. "Just so everyone knows, I'll be wearing it during the upcoming singing contest."

The man cast a warm smile. "I couldn't help but overhear the lovely singing." He looked at me and said, "Granted, with such a lovely face, to go along with such a beautiful voice, you'd be sure to win."

Beatrice stepped in between me and the man, then patted her chest. "It was me! It was my voice you heard." She raised her chin. "I'm the one with the beautiful voice." She turned and squinted at me. "Why, she's is just an ordinary maid servant, and I might say, a pretty poor one at that." She handed me a broom. "What chance would she have at winning anything?" She took a deep breath and sang a short tune to show off her vocal talents.

The delivery man smiled. "Well then… the best of luck to the four… I mean, three of you."

Paula swayed her head side to side. "Luck? Luck! What you do you mean, 'luck'?" she said, slamming the door in his face. "The nerve of that man."

******

While I prepared breakfast the next morning,

the three sisters were busy upstairs getting dressed in preparation for the singing contest.

A short time later, while I was busy serving the sisters their breakfast, I heard a sudden knock by the back door. When I opened it, a bearded man wearing an old looking blue suit and red top hat introduce himself to me as Mr. Pepper, the pastries man.

Gilda leaned back in her chair and peered down the hallway. "Who is it, maid?"

"It's Mr. Pepper, the pastries man."

He took out one of his boxes, opened it, and showed me a sample of his donuts.

I looked back over my shoulder toward the sisters. "He has lots of sweet donuts with him."

Beatrice's eyes suddenly stretched wide. "Ah! Sweets. Let him in. Let's have a look-see."

The instant Mr. Pepper reached the dining table, Beatrice reached out and grabbed a box of sweets from his hands.

There were an assortment colors and flavors of to choose from: pink strawberry flavor, chocolate, vanilla with rainbow sugar sprinkles, and much more.

Beatrice helped herself. "I'll take this one, and that one, and that one." She hesitated a moment, then grabbed one more. "Oh, I can't resist that one too, but that's all." She handed what was left in the box back to the man, then gave him a smile. "I'm on a strict diet, you know." She held the plate of donuts up to her nose and inhaled deeply. "I have to watch what I eat... at least until I win the singing contest and marry Prince Arnold." She put her hand over her mouth and giggled. "Then I can get back to eating a dozen donuts a day."

I thought that perhaps she might have a chance at winning the contest if the prince preferred sugar-coated songs.

Gilda picked out a small donut. "Yes, this chocolate one will do quite nicely. Yes, indeed."

Mr. Pepper smiled ear-to-ear. "Come now, that's not enough to even feed a mouse," he said, handing her a fresh box to choose from.

Mr. Pepper looked my way and gave me a big smile. "Is this young lass in the contest, too?"

Beatrice squinted at Mr. Pepper. "What, Hailee, the maid servant? Hah... what a silly thought."

Paula pointed at me with her cheeks stuffed with a strawberry flavored donut. "Yes," she muttered, with bits of donut popping out from her mouth as she spoke. "Hailee is only fit to cook, clean dishes, and mop floors."

"I had a daughter who died of the fever," said Mr. Pepper. "She looked just like Hailee. And not only that, she had the most beautiful singing voice in all the land."

Gilda shook her head. "Well...too bad she died. Now you'll never know if she ever had a chance against us."

Mr. Pepper's head sunk low and his eyes swelled with tears.

I thought, *Those sisters are so cruel.*

After seeing Mr. Pepper off, I stood by the front porch and watched the three sisters' step into their carriage.

Gilda stuck her head out the carriage window and pointed at me. "Remember maid, we expect every bit of our clothes in the bedroom ironed perfect before we get back." Her eyebrows sank low. "Understand?"

I nodded and gave her a forced smile.

She waved at me. "That's right maid. Stay happy, and work hard, always."

Easy for her to say, I though, not having to lift a finger for a second's worth of work, except maybe to polish her cracked fingernails.

I watched the carriage driver take the three sisters merrily on their way to the royal singing event.

CHAPTER 29

I opened the upstairs window, looked out toward the castle, and wondered; if I had a beautiful dress, perhaps I too could attend the singing contest, and have a chance at winning.

I tried to think of something to cheer me up while ironing the sisters' clothes, so I started to sing one of the beautiful songs Higgins taught me. As I sang, I glanced out the window and saw Mr. Pepper on the other side of the road selling more of his donuts. He suddenly stopped what he was doing and watched me sing. The moment I finished my song, he gave me a big smile, clapped his hands, then hurried across the street toward the sisters' house.

Seconds later, I heard a sudden knock on

the front door. I hurried downstairs and saw Mr. Pepper standing on the front porch.

"I heard the most enchanting voice, so beautiful, so sweet," he said, giving me a big smile. "When I looked back to see who it was, there you were, singing out the upstairs window." He clasped his palms together in front of him, as if in prayer, and said, "I think you stand a chance at winning the singing contest. I really do."

I laughed. "Surely, you must be joking. I haven't been singing that long, and besides, how could I ever have a chance against so many talented contestants?"

He pointed at me. "Be confident. I truly believe that you have the most beautiful voice in all the land." He looked up and down the road. "Many a voice has filled the streets of this town, but I dare say, never such a one as yours."

I shook my head. "But I have so little experience compared to all the other singers."

He smiled, then pointed his finger toward his head. "It's all up here. Believe in yourself. I believe in you!"

I held my hands out in front of me. "But I don't know anything about the contest."

"The king of Nod, of the kingdom of Bore, is trying to find the maiden with the most beautiful singing voice in all the land to become a princess for his son, Prince Arnold. The King put out a decree across the land, and even in faraway lands about the contest. He called for beautiful maidens everywhere to come attend. Whosoever receives the greatest applause in the concert hall for the most beautiful voice will become princess to Prince Arnold, in the land of Nod, kingdom of Bore."

I giggled, thinking it kind of funny to name the kingdom "Bore," so I asked him why.

"Hailee, nearly everyone in the city upon rising from their beds, nods their heads and yawns in boredom. During breakfast, they would nod and yawn. In the afternoon, they would yawn. And in the evening, they would yawn, in the land of Nod, kingdom of Bore."

I said, "Even if I wanted to attend, I couldn't." I looked down at my plain maid's clothes and funny-looking green shoes with the squared-off front. "I could never go there looking like this. It wouldn't be right to attend the contest dressed in these clothes."

He glanced at me from head to toe, then smiled. "Yes, it might work. I think you to be about the same size. Yes, I think it could be a perfect fit."

"Perfect fit?"

"My daughter would want you to have it."

"Have what?"

"Her dress. I want you to take her place of honor at the King's singing contest. Please do it for my daughter."

"I couldn't."

He gave me a serious look. "Oh please, please, wear it. If not for me, then for my daughter. In her memory."

"Well... all right." I gave him a puzzled look. "But what about the invitation? How could I attend without one?"

Mr. Pepper grinned. "Oh, we'll work on that problem when we get there. Hurry up now, and get cleaned up while I fetch the dress and get my buggy."

I rushed upstairs to the bedroom and borrowed one of the sister's combs to brush my hair.

I thought it was so nice for Mr. Pepper to have such confidence in my singing ability. I hoped that I had a chance at winning the contest, just like he said.

Minutes later, I heard a knock at the front door. I ran downstairs and saw Mr. Pepper standing on the porch with his arms extended, holding a glittering emerald-green dress, red velvet belt, and pretty pink bonnet decorated with a fluffy white ostrich feather that curved around the front. "Here, take these and put them on."

I couldn't believe how beautiful the dress, belt and hat looked. "They're wonderful. Thank you so very much!"

"I'm glad you approve. Hurry now. Get inside and put them on. No time to waste. Not a second to lose."

I ran upstairs and put the dress on in the sisters' room. A pile of clothes was still left on the bed for me to iron. I hoped and prayed that by some miracle this would be the last time I would ever see those clothes again. Whether I won the contest or not, I figured I would be out of the house and on my own.

I ran out the front door and across the cobblestone pathway, then stepped up onto the buggy seat next to Mr. Pepper.

His buggy was a far cry from the fancy carriage the sisters rode in, and not much to look at, but it was more than adequate, I thought, to get us where we needed to go in a hurry.

"Giddy-up," said Mr. Pepper, with a sharp jerk on the reins. His horse must have gotten the message that we were in a hurry, because he took off like he was in a real race against time.

I felt so relieved the moment the castle finally came into view. A wide moat surrounded its towering walls of stone.

Our buggy raced toward the bridge, leading to the castle entrance. Right as we were about to cross the bridge, my heart sank low seeing the drawbridge suddenly rise shut before us. I sighed deeply, and thought, *Could it be that we traveled such a long distance, with such a great promise of hope, only to be turned away at the last moment?*

Seconds later, our carriage stopped in front of the drawbridge. I looked up and saw two towers on either side of the main gate with guards pacing back and forth on each.

Mr. Pepper stood up on the buggy, cupped his hands around his mouth and shouted out to one of the guards, "The king has one more contestant! Lower the bridge. Let her join the others!"

The guard peered down at us. "Sorry. Strict rules. No contestants past three o'clock."

Mr. Pepper turned and looked me straight in the eye, "Sing, Hailee. Sing like you never sang before."

A couple minutes after I started to sing I saw a man dressed in a beautiful green robe suddenly appear at the top of the castle wall. He stared down at me with a smile on his face that grew larger by the second. I could hardly believe it when, a minute later, I saw the drawbridge suddenly lower before us.

One of the guards led me to a private dressing room so I could fix my wind-blown hair. As I tidied myself up in front of a gold-framed mirror, a bright ball of light suddenly appeared behind me that grew larger by the second. A beautiful angel stepped out from the light; the same angel I had seen that one night back in cave when I was still the Mushroom Monster. I remembered the words she spoke to me then: "When your pain becomes so great you think you cannot bear it, you will have unspeakable joy, if you endure the trials, keep the faith, and live a life in love and kindness for others."

The angel moved closer, with her face aglow, and said, "Remember when you first found your voice and scared away the bear?"

I nodded and said, "Yes, I remember every moment, all too well."

She pointed toward the door, in the direction of the concert hall. "Just like that time, you will now be facing a crowd of bears today in competition to win the prince's hand. After singing, you will suffer unspeakable pain, but be strong, and take courage my child. Sing again like you did before the bear, with all your might, and all will be well. All will be well."

I gave her a puzzled look. "But won't that hurt their ears?"

"Never mind, my child. Trust me." The angel stepped back toward the ball of light while repeating her message, "Be brave, take courage, and all will be well. All will be well." A moment later, she entered the glowing ball of light, then vanished into thin air.

******

As I headed down the hallway, I glanced to my left and saw three stone archways leading to the concert hall already filled with hundreds of guests awaiting the start of the contest.

I felt so nervous knowing that not long from now I would be singing before that same crowd of people.

I headed through a stone hallway to join the other contestants. On my way, I passed by colored flags representing the different countries from which the maidens came.

I got in line behind a row of fifty contestants all arrayed in fine dresses. Their hair shined and looked so beautiful. Many had styled their hair in curls that bounced every time they turned their head, or took a step. I wondered how I could ever compete against such talent and beauty. I thought that if their voices were even half as beautiful as their looks, I didn't know how I would ever stand a chance at winning.

I heard a voice that struck fear in my heart. It sounded like one the three sisters. *Oh no,* I thought. *What will happen if they see me here competing against them?* They expected me to be at home ironing their clothes. I stood directly behind the contestant in front of me and tried to keep myself hidden. I leaned slightly to one side and glanced down the row of ladies. Yes, there they were. I could see them clearly. The three sisters were standing toward the front of the line, chatting, laughing and giggling between themselves.

Gilda suddenly looked my way. I hoped she didn't see me. I waited a minute, then took a peek around the lady in front of me. Gilda hadn't moved, and was still staring at me. I thought, *Oh no, what am I going to do now?* Perhaps she didn't recognize me in my beautiful dress and hat. I decided to take one more peek. My heart dropped when I saw her leave her sisters' place in line and walk toward me. When she got closer, her mouth suddenly dropped open. I felt sure she recognized me now. She hurried back to her sisters and whispered into their ears. The next thing I knew, all three of them were staring back at me with bulging eyes. I pretended I didn't notice them and looked the other way.

A minute later, I felt a sudden tap on my shoulder. When I turned to see who it was, I found myself face-to-face with my worst nightmare; the three sisters. They stood next to me in silence with their mouths hanging wide open, all the while staring at my shoes, dress, and feathered hat.

Gilda's eyebrows cringed. "What are "*YOU*" doing here?" she screeched, pointing at my face.

Paula gave me a mean look. "How did you sneak into the castle?"

Beatrice poked my shoulder. "Who gave you permission to leave the house without finishing the ironing? There's no way you could have finished all our clothes this early. You are officially fired!" She pointed down the hallway toward the exit. "Out in the street with you, girl." She raised her chin. "See how long that dress lasts while digging in the trash for food."

Gilda gave me a snarling face. "Yes, out in the street with you. Do you think after word gets out about your un-trustworthy maid habits anyone else will ever hire you again?" She turned, faced her sisters, and said, "Cleaning chimneys would be a better job for her. Don't you think so, sisters?"

They nodded.

Paula pointed and laughed at me. "Are you the king's jester? You're the biggest joke. You really need to be getting back to the house now and finish ironing our clothes, then maybe, just maybe, we might consider keeping you as our maid." She pointed her finger at my nose. "We never gave you permission to stop ironing. Did we? Well, answer us! Did we?"

I stood in front of them in silence, with a straight face, trying to take all their abuse without lashing back and causing a big scene in front of all the other contestants.

Beatrice shook her head at me. "Do you think you have a chance against me? Against us? The magnificent threesome?" she asked, raising her chin high, while pointing at her chest. "Really now, what were you thinking, coming here like this? Why, you're just an ordinary maid, fit only to wash and clean floors and dishes." She grinned. "And where did you get that dreadful looking outfit?" She shook her head, and stared at my dress. "Do you really think you can go onstage wearing that?"

I sighed with my head sunk low in despair. It was almost unbearable to have to listen to their cruel words for such a long a time. Just then, I felt a surge of confidence, remembering the angel's words of encouragement to me. Mr. Pepper had given me a lot of confidence too, telling me that I stood a good chance at winning the contest.

"Go home," snarled Gilda, waving me away. "You're not even invited, or on the royal list of singers." She asked Paula to give her the brochure, then held it up to my face. "See! Look here. Do you see your name anywhere? Do you? Well, do you!" She moved the list closer.

I gave her a confused look. I couldn't understand all the words, but didn't want them to know that.

"Can't you read?" said Beatrice, grabbing the brochure from her sister's hand. "I'll show you." Her eyes glanced down the list of names. A second later her mouth suddenly dropped open in shock. "No it can't be," she said. "I don't believe it." She exchanged glances between the paper, her sisters, and me. "Impossible." She shook her head. "I don't know how, but her name has been added."

Beatrice pointed out my name to her sisters, the last one on the list. She chuckled. "This must be a joke?"

They huddled in a circle, staring at my name with narrowed eyes.

Paula pointed at a sentence written below my

name. "And what's this?"

"What, sister?"asked Gilda.

Paula chuckled. "There's a sentence written underneath her name that says, 'When your pain becomes so great you cannot bear it, clap as hard as you can.'"

Beatrice laughed. "What a silly thing to say. I wonder if this might be the work of the king's jester."

Paula's nose wrinkled. "Certainly, it must be the jester's joke."

Beatrice laughed. "Yes, who else would make such a foolish remark like that?"

CHAPTER 30

The trumpets sounded, announcing the start of the royal singing event. The three sisters rushed back to their places in line and faced straight ahead with the other contestants.

All the singers lined up on stage, faced the audience, then gave their name and country from whence they came.

This was the first time I was able to catch a glimpse of Prince Arnold. I thought that he was quite a handsome man, with his shoulder length black hair, dimpled chin, and ice blue eyes.

After the brief introductions, the contestants were directed offstage and instructed to wait to have their names called.

A girl named Brandi McLean was the first one called to come forward and sing. Her flowing white dress trailed across the floor behind her like a beautiful wedding gown. I figured, if by chance she won the contest, she wouldn't even have to change her dress to marry the prince. I loved her red velvet cape and gold-striped purple hat, accented with a large white feather that curved around the front. My hat had a white feather just like hers. When she got onstage, she announced that she would be singing a song called, "I Remember, I Remember" by Thomas Hood. In addition to selecting a lovely song, I thought that her voice was very unique and sweet.

Right after she finished, she received a standing ovation, and very loud applause. I thought it would be difficult for the contestants who came after her to match her performance and level of applause.

The second contestant to be called onstage was a beautiful red-haired lady named Christine Bower. She was dressed in a green and white dress and a black, long-sleeved felt shirt. She announced the name of her song, "Things Love Thee, So Do I," by Anon, composed by Charles Edward Horn. Her voice was crisp and clear, and her words seemed to flutter upon the air as she sang.

When Christine finished her song, she received a very strong applause. I think it would be very close to the applause received by Brandi.

Beatrice, one of the three sisters, and Mr. Pepper's best donut customer, was called up next to give her best performance. She sashayed onstage with her chin raised high. When she reached center stage, she turned and faced the audience with a smile that stretched from ear to ear.

For this special occasion, Beatrice wore her pleated red velvet dress with royal blue stripes. Her white bonnet was decorated with a pink netted fabric, a purple bow, and a half dozen miniature yellow roses.

She started to sing a song I heard her practice several times back at the house called "Highland Mary," lyrics by Robert Burns. Her voice was loud and a little bit sour. Several times during the song she turned and batted her eyelashes at Prince Arnold, giving him her biggest donut smile, which I have to admit, looked pretty sweet.

When Beatrice finished her song, she received a nice applause, but I think not as strong as the previous contestants, and I think she knew it too. She pouted and shed tears like a big baby. I thought, *What a loser!*

Beatrice's other sisters followed, and had their chance to sing. All three of them received a nice applause, but I think not as loud as the singers who sang before them. I heard them argue between themselves who they thought got the loudest applause, and who amongst them won the contest. I thought, *What dreamers!*

One by one, about every ten minutes, I heard a new contestant called forward to give their best performance. I heard many beautiful voices, and lots of applause at the end of each. With so many singers, it was hard for me to know who got the biggest applause.

Finally, the moment had arrived when I heard my name called to go onstage. The sisters stood just behind the side curtain as I approached. They pointed, snickered, and giggled at me with their hands covering their mouth. Gilda suddenly stuck her foot out in front of me, and I experienced a dreadful feeling of falling forward, with no way to keep my balance. A second later I found myself spread flat across the stage with my head turned sideways, facing the audience. Everyone burst out laughing. I glanced back and saw Gilda point at me with her nose raised so high, the holes in her nostrils reminded me of a laughing pig in a fancy dress.

I felt so angry and humiliated. I knew Gilda was a mean hearted person, but to trip me like that was devilish. It was hard enough as it was to get the courage to go onstage, and now this? I felt like running toward the exit, but instead got back up and tried to regain my composure. With so many people giggling and laughing at me, I found it very difficult to take the remaining five steps to the center stage. My legs felt unsteady and shaky as I faced an audience of over three hundred laughing spectators. The King and Prince looked sore displeased by their laughing, and frowned at the crowd. The room suddenly fell silent, and the audience glared back at me with varied expressions, ranging from pouts to wide smiles. I took a deep breath, closed my eyes for a moment, and remembered the angel's last words to me: "Be brave, take courage, and all will be well, all will be well."

I put on a big smile and started to sing one of the beautiful songs Higgins taught me, which just also happened to be my favorite called, "Amazing Grace." The words seemed to flow out of my mouth sweet as honey as I sang. I glanced to my right, and through the corner of my eye, saw Prince Arnold give me a smile and nod of approval. I felt lighter than air at that moment. Glancing the other way,

I saw the three sisters glaring back at me with wrinkled noses. Gilda raised her chin and pinched her nose at me.

I felt very happy the way the song was going, and found it quite easy to ignore the three sisters. I believed that if I remained focused on my song until the end I might even be able to receive an applause greater than Brandi, whom I thought to be the lead singer. When I finished my song, I felt a surge of confidence, and truly believed that I had a real chance at winning the contest.

I bowed, then cast a big smile before the crowd, believing with all my heart that I would receive an applause so loud, it would be greater than anyone else who sang before me. But my smile quickly dropped, and heart sank low, for I couldn't believe what I was hearing, or "*not*" hearing, to be exact. The only thing I could hear was the light tapping of hands, a far cry from a real applause. Only Mr. Pepper, who was sitting in the last row, applauded loudly with a big smile on his face. For the rest of the audience, they looked so bored, and stared at me with faces that didn't show any emotion at all. Not even a grin.

Beatrice pointed and laughed at me. "I told you so." I heard her sisters join in, laughing along with her.

My head, shoulders, and just about everything else about me slumped low in sadness. I didn't know if I could ever look back into the sea of faces again. Perhaps they thought my song was nice, but couldn't get out of their mind the clumsy contestant, who just moments earlier, tripped flat on her face before them.

I felt great sorrow at that moment. So much so I didn't think I could bear the pain a moment longer. Just then, I remembered what the angel told me about suffering unspeakable pain, but to remain strong and take courage. Her other words came to my remembrance as well. "Sing again, like you did before the bear, with all your might, and with all your strength, and all will be well." Those words didn't seem to make that much sense to me, but I felt confident in the angel's instructions, and besides, I had nothing else to lose.

I raised my head, closed my eyes, and pictured myself during that horrific moment in time when the bear stood before me and I thought that my life would be taken away. Next, I started to make the same high-pitched notes I did before the bear. As a matter of fact, I felt myself singing in a higher pitch than I did then. Everyone's hands instantly flew up to cover their ears. One high note after the other flowed out from my mouth. Then it happened. I saw two stain glass windows along the back wall shatter and rain pieces of glass upon the floor.

It appeared as though everyone couldn't bear to hear my high notes much longer. I saw several people in the crowd stare down at their brochure a moment, then start to applaud loudly. They in turn pointed at the brochure to the people sitting next to them, and seconds later, they applauded as well. Moments later, everyone in the audience was applauding so loud it drowned out my voice, so I decided to stop. It looked as if everyone in the audience was smiling now, relieved that I stopped my high-pitched singing.

CHAPTER 31

All fifty contestants walked back on stage, lined up, then faced the audience. I gazed to my left and saw the singers give their biggest smiles to the crowd, each one hoping to be called up front as the winner.

The seven contest judges got up from their chairs and huddled in a circle. They must have had differences of opinion as to who won, because we had to wait for several minutes before they wrote down the name of the winner. King Henry and Prince Arnold glanced at the name written on the parchment, smiled, then gave their nod of approval.

One of the King's magistrates, dressed in a gold robe, studded with colored gems, and a silver cross necklace, stepped on stage carrying the foot-long parchment. He faced the audience a moment, then glanced down and started to read, "According to the rules of the contest decreed by King Henry, the maid receiving the loudest applause will become princess of the land of Nod, kingdom of Bore, and wed Prince Arnold." He looked up, and stared across the sea of faces a moment, cleared his throat, then looked back at the parchment. "The decree doesn't specify the means by which a contestant shall attain the loudest applause, only that she receives it. Thus, hereby, after much consideration, the magistrates have decided upon a winner." He turned and smiled at me. "Congratulations Hailee Tupper! Please step forward."

When the three sisters heard my name called, they stepped out of line and stomped toward me with the ugliest, meanest, faces they could dream up.

Gilda turned and pointed at me. "She's a cheat!"

Beatrice stood next to her sister. "Yes, she's a cheat and didn't play fair!"

Paula got her word in too. "She doesn't belong here! We're the greatest I tell you! Not her!" she shouted, pointing at herself and two sisters. "There has been a terrible, terrible mistake!"

The King pointed at his guards, then at the

sisters. The guards hurried onstage, grabbed the sisters by their arms, then forcefully escorted them away. Everyone continued to hear their rants and screams until they were completely removed from the concert hall.

I had to pinch myself to make sure I wasn't dreaming.

King Henry and Prince Arnold stepped onstage. The King stood next to me and said, "My daughter, neither I, nor my son, could be more delighted for such a glorious moment as this." I heard several trumpets sound off. A man wearing a red robe stepped behind me and placed a gold crown upon my head.

I couldn't believe what I was seeing and hearing. Everyone in the audience stood up and repeated the magistrate's words with one accord, 'Hail to Princess Hailee! Hail to Princess Hailee!'

The King had me and the prince clasp hands, then said, "My son, you are blessed this day not only to find the maiden with the most beautiful voice in all the land to marry, but also one that possesses the face of an angel. My blessings be upon you both." That being said, he looped a red and white silk ribbon around our hands. The audience applauded loudly.

I felt as if the angel's words of prophesy

concerning my life was now fulfilled in a more miraculous way than I could have ever possibly imagined. I'll always remember her words to me; "When your pain becomes so great you think you cannot bear it, you will have unspeakable joy, if you endure the trials, keep the faith, and live a life in love and kindness for others."

I was so thankful to God for my guardian angel and her message of hope for a better future. I really believe now more than ever before in the power of prayer and miracles. Who could have ever imagined that I, once a horrible-looking monster, could be so transformed, win the hand of the king's son, and become a princess.

From that day forward, everyone seemed to smile, bow, or curtsy before me. I couldn't imagine such a life as I have now. I really had unspeakable joy.

I was so very happy with my new life as princess, no longer having to look back over my shoulder and worry about anyone speaking unkind words, or throwing rotten food at me.

Although I felt much joy, deep inside I also felt great emptiness, knowing that there were so many other people outside the castle and beyond who were in need of special help, love, and compassion. I decided that I was going to do something for the good of mankind. I also wanted animals not to suffer. I wanted to help them in anyway I could. I wanted them to be treated with compassion, feel truly loved, and not go hungry. I wanted to keep everyone from experiencing the life that I had to suffer for so many years. As princess of the land of Nod, kingdom of Bore, I now had the power, money, and influence to start programs everywhere designed to help take care of the poor, needy, and unfortunate souls who were born far from perfect, like me.

With the grace and strength coming from God, I was able to start organizations like; the Bore Public Library, staffed with teachers ready and willing to help anyone learn how to read and write; the Nod Orphan Society, to care for kids who were without parents and all alone; the Sisters of Bore Charity, designed to raise money worldwide to help feed and provide shelter for those in need; the Nod School for the Deaf and Mute, and the Bore House of Refuge, to help train and take care of anyone born with a deformity, or has special needs like I had growing up.

Prince Arnold inquired if I had any other wishes. I told him that it was my wish to visit the land of my birth and try to find my parents. I also wanted to see my dear friend Higgins, who taught me so many wonderful things about life, like faith, hope, courage, miracles and beautiful songs.

I told Prince Arnold all about my tiger friend, Zebu, and that I wanted to find out if he was still alive. I also requested that a special decree be put forth across the land to look for a very special dog named Brutus. I told my Prince about Captain Graze, and how he mistreated me and Brutus. When he heard that, his smile suddenly soured. He walked alongside me with his arm wrapped around my shoulder and reassured me that he would personally take care of Captain Graze for the cruel way he treated me and Brutus.

Not wanting to get revenge, I had my husband promise me not to do physical harm to Captain Graze. He said not to worry, and that he would discipline him in an orderly, but not cruel manner.

Two weeks later, I received fantastic news! I was informed that one of the King's ships, dubbed, The Bore Wind, was provisioned and ready to set sail to take me back to my homeland. I wasted no time in packing my belongings for the long voyage home. After giving my husband a big hug and kiss, I departed for the ship.

When I arrived at the dock, I stepped down from the carriage and looked up toward the top of the boarding ramp. I blinked and rubbed my eyes in disbelief. I just couldn't believe what I was seeing! My beloved dog Brutus was staring back at me from the top of the ramp, wagging his tail like crazy. *They found my precious Brutus!* I could hardly believe it! I sprinted up the ramp as fast as my legs could carry me. Brutus raced a quarter of the way down, then took a flying leap into my arms. I gave him a smothering hug and kiss.

I noticed that someone was staring down at me from the top deck who looked very familiar. I just couldn't remember exactly who he was, that is, until he smiled and I saw some missing teeth on the side of his mouth. It was Captain Graze, no longer in a captain's uniform, but instead he was a clean-shaven man, dressed as a waiter, wearing a tall chef's hat, holding a platter of meaty bones, which I soon discovered were for Brutus.

One of the crew hands stepped up to me and whispered into my ear, "Prince Arnold stripped Graze of his rank as Captain, he did. Ordered him to be Brutus's personal waiter, and follow him where he be goin'. Every hour that lucky dog gets a juicy bone of his choosin.'"

I bet Brutus had many a bone to pick with the former Captain Graze. It was no wonder Brutus appeared to be so happy. His stubby tail couldn't stop wagging. I thought he looked healthier now than I had ever seen him in the past. Even his coat appeared to glisten from the reflection of sunlight.

When I walked past Chef Graze, I smelled something not so pleasant about him. It was a different kind of smell than I remembered him having, since the last time I saw him inside "The Salty Cracker." I was told that after Brutus finished eating, Chef Graze was ordered by Prince Arnold to take off his shoe and catch Brutus's pee after each meal, then empty the not-so-precious golden cargo over the side of the ship.

Now I knew where the smell was coming from. It was from his stinky shoes. I thought Prince Arnold did a pretty good job at humbling the former Captain Graze and in teaching him the importance of kindness, humility, and servitude.

Unlike the other ship hands who were required to spend a certain amount of time cleaning the deck, Chef Graze was ordered to clean his stinky shoes in a large wooden bucket. I had to cover my mouth to keep from laughing when I saw Brutus sitting and staring up at Chef Graze with what looked like a smile on his face while watching him scrub his shoes in the bucket of soapy water.

CHAPTER 32

After spending many days at sea, and sailing through both calm and stormy weather, I heard the sailor in the crow's nest shout, "Land ahoy! Land ahoy!" I rushed toward the bow of the boat and squinted out through the white mist. I was so happy to see the Brunsville Harbor finally come into view. Minutes later, the helmsman steered our ship through the narrow channel into port.

After getting a good night's rest from the long voyage at sea, I got up early the next morning and took a carriage ride to the Brunsville Zoo.

I was so excited knowing that in just a few short minutes I would be meeting my beloved friend Higgins, and hopefully Zebu and Igor as well. I walked down the zoo pathway and approached the three caves I remembered in the past: the tiger, the gorilla, and the one that used to be my home when I was still the Mushroom Monster. I saw a large tiger roaming around the first exhibit. I thought, *Could it possibly be my friend, Zebu?* I ran down the pathway, then leaned over the railing and called out to him. The tiger stopped and stared at me a moment. A slight breeze blew my scent his direction, and the tiger immediately walked toward me. He stopped and stared at me a moment, then suddenly leaped into the air, acting as if he just found his long lost friend. Next, he paced back and forth in front of the moat, all the while keeping his eyes fixed on my every move. I realized, right then and there, that it must be my beloved tiger friend, Zebu. I could clearly see by his reaction that he recognized me now. I was so happy to see him looking so healthy and well fed.

I didn't see Higgins make his rounds yet, so I decided to check out my old cave exhibit. I was very surprised to see the old "Mushroom Monster" sign still hanging above the cave opening. I thought, *They should have found another animal to put in the exhibit by now.*

The moment I walked over to the gorilla exhibit, my mouth dropped open and eyes stretched wide seeing my dear friend Igor step out of his cave. He stretched his arms above his head, gave a big yawn, then beat his chest. When

I called out to him, he just gave me a blank stare at first, probably thinking that I was just another zoo visitor. But when I raised my hand and gave him the "V" for victory sign, he ran right over and sat on the grass in front of me. He acted like he wanted to play some games, so we entertained each other a few minutes by taking turns beating our chests and scratching under our armpits, just like we did before.

I felt so glad for Igor and Zebu, especially since they both appeared to be so healthy and happy. They must have been feeding them much better since I left.

I was surprised to see as many as fifty people rushing down the zoo pathway. When they got within ten feet of me, they suddenly turned and faced what used to be the Mushroom Monster exhibit. I thought, *What could possibly be more interesting than seeing Zebu or Igor?*

A minute later, even more people gathered in front of the exhibit that used to be my cave. They looked impatient, and started to shout for the monster to come out. I walked up to a lady with three children and said, "I'm sorry, but the Mushroom Monster vanished without a trace several months ago."

The lady gave me a puzzled look. "You're

dearly mistaken. We saw her just of last week, we did."

I gave her a confused look. "The Mushroom Monster?"

She nodded. "She is due to be showing her monster face in just a moment. Just you wait and see." Her daughter looked up at me with wide stretched eyes. "She's a big monster. A terrible looking one."

I wondered if Miss Finch found another poor, deformed child to take my place. I sure hoped that wasn't the case.

CHAPTER 33

I was shocked to see someone step out of the Mushroom Monster cave with a face so disfigured she almost didn't look human. For a moment I thought they had found a real life monster for the exhibit. When she moved closer, I gasped in horror! The monster's arms and legs could only belong to one person. Someone I knew for many years. It was Miss Finch! I couldn't believe it! She looked horrible! Just then, I had a flashback to that horrible evening when Zebu sunk his teeth into her leg, then leaped on top of her, pawing at her face over and over again. I could plainly see the scar left on her calf from his bite. Zebu must have unleashed all his built up hatred toward her for all the cruelty she inflicted on him, and in the process, tore her face up so bad, she ended up looking like a monster.

A boy in his early teens, wearing a red cap, yelled at Miss Finch. "You're a horrible looking beast!"

An old lady raised her cane and pointed it at her. "You're an ogre! The ugliest person on earth!"

I raised my hands and covered my ears to keep from hearing those hurtful words. They brought back horrible memories from the time when I was standing in her place. As cruel as she was to me, I would never have wished this upon her, even after the many years of horrible treatment I suffered under her care.

A boy about eight years old stood next to me and pulled out a rotten tomato from a brown paper bag. With the veggie firmly in his grasp, he locked eyes with Miss Finch, then arched the tomato back across his shoulder. I quickly reached down and snatched it out of his hand just in the nick of time to keep it from flying over the fence and hitting Miss Finch. I squinted at the boy and said, "Even monsters deserve better than that."

Before I knew it, another child in the crowd threw a tomato over the fence, hitting Miss Finch's chest. I shook my head seeing tomato seeds, skin and juice splatter up and down her neck and stomach. That same moment, I heard someone clapping loudly as if they really enjoyed seeing that. When I turned to see who was doing the clapping I was shocked to see that it was Igor the gorilla! I gave him a frown and told him to stop it. I bet Igor remembered all the cruel things Miss Finch did to me and Zebu in the past, and somehow thought it was now entertaining to see food thrown at her instead.

I'm so thankful to Higgins for teaching me the importance of being forgiving, even to such a mean person as Miss Finch. I felt so much at peace now, being able to forgive. For all the years of torture under her care, I should have much hatred toward her, but instead, I only felt pity.

I saw a nice looking loaf of bread sticking part way out of a picnic basket a lady was holding beside me. She agreed to sell it to me after I offered her twice what it cost her. I looked through the fence, cupped my hands around my mouth, and shouted, "Miss Finch!" The moment she looked my way, I tossed the loaf of bread over the fence. In midair she must have recognized it as a nice, unspoiled piece of food, because she ran forward and somehow was able to catch it before it hit the ground. She cradled the loaf in her arms like it was a baby, then gave me a smile. I didn't think she recognized me yet, but looked as if she appreciated the food I gave her.

"Go ahead monster," shouted a young man, "Let's see you swallow the whole loaf with one bite!"

Miss Finch's smile vanished, and I could see tears swell in her eyes, then roll down the sides of her face.

I heard a man call out through the crowd, "Let's move along now. Let other people have a chance to be seein' the monster."

I instantly recognized that voice. It was my dear friend Higgins. I ran over and gave him a big hug and kiss on the cheek, but he stepped back, acting as if he was just kissed by a complete stranger.

I gave him a big smile. "It's me. Hailee... Hailee Tupper. That's what you said my name was when I was still the Mushroom Monster."

He looked away a moment, chuckled, and then glanced back at me like I was crazy. "Impossible. Even if there be such a miracle, I couldn't be believin' she could be so beautiful, and a princess at that."

I thought to myself, what else could I say that only the Mushroom Monster would know? I remembered some things he told me about his family. "You have four brothers and five sisters and your parents were so poor that you had to help support the family by working at Montgomery Textiles. Um... now I remember, you also said that your boss's name was Mr. Peabody. You never got a formal education, but you were still able to teach me about the outside world through your sketches, and later, beautiful paintings. You also learned many beautiful songs growing up. There was one *special song* you taught me that I hold close to my heart, and will always remember." I gave him the "V" for victory sign and started to sing "Amazing Grace."

Higgins dropped to his knees before me and wept. I immediately reached down and lifted him up. "Don't kneel. I'm no one special."

Tears beaded down his face. "Could there possibly be such a miracle, that the Mushroom Monster could change, to be one such as you?"

I reached out and placed my hand on his shoulder. "You taught me something very important, and that is to have faith and believe in miracles." I pointed toward the sky. "You told me that if I gazed up into the stars at night and continued in prayer, and really believed that a miracle could happen, it would someday. Well... a miracle did happen, and changed my life forever."

He stepped up to me, placed his face close

to mine, then stared deeply into my eyes, the window of my soul, just like he did on the day I was born when he said that he saw something precious and dear beneath the outer layer of my moldy mushroom self. After a moment of silence, I saw a hint of a grin on his face, which quickly grew into a big smile. "It's a miracle indeed. Yes... I do believe now. It be really you."

I gave him a hug and said, "I have a special request."

"Yes, what could it be?"

"I would like to see if I you could help me find my parents."

Higgins sighed. "I learned after you be gone that Miss Finch offered money to your parents, she did, so that they would be movin' to a bigger house far away from here."

I shook my head. "But why?"

"Greed. The extra salary she got for bringing you here. Crowds came to see you, they did. Everyone wanted to buy tickets. The Mushroom Monster exhibit became popular, it did. Miss Finch couldn't chance your parents be discovering what she did with you."

"Wouldn't she tell you where my parents moved to?"

Higgins shook his head. "No, many times I be

pleading her for such, but she always refused."

"At least I know that my parents might still be alive, and there's still a chance to find them. I have to convince her to show me where they are."

He shook his head. "There be little hope of that."

"I'm counting on one more miracle, and that is to find my parents. I'm not giving up, no matter what. Miss Finch is the only one who knows where they are now." I gazed toward Miss Finch and sighed. "How did she get locked inside the exhibit like that?"

"Mr. Brunsky, the zoo owner, hot-tempered he was, when you disappeared, then the tiger cub too. He blamed Miss Finch for both, he did. Put her behind bars to replace you, he did. She be the new Mushroom Monster now."

"I would like to have a word with Mr. Brunsky. Can you take me to his office?"

Higgins nodded. "Follow me."

He led me up along the zoo pathway to a white building located on a hill overlooking the zoo.

Shortly thereafter, I found myself sitting in a black leather coach inside the zoo owner's office.

Mr. Brunsky stepped into the room and seated himself behind his black oval desk. He was a well-rounded man, sporting a stubby mustache, and shiny bald head.

"Well now, what can I do for you?" he asked, leaning forward in his chair.

"I wish to have Miss Finch released from the Brunsville Zoo at once."

He grinned and shook his head. "Out of the question."

Mr. Brunsky rejected two more pleas for her release, but when I offered him a large sum of money, he suddenly had a change of heart, and agreed to let her go.

I told him that I'm having an inspector visit his zoo from time to time to make sure all of the animals are treated well. I also informed him to take extra good care of my dear friends, Igor the gorilla, and the tiger I named Zebu.

My final message to him was that a prison sentence awaits anyone caught trying to sell any animal to a game reserve to he hunted for sport.

******

Higgins unlocked the door to my old exhibit, then walked through the cave to the grass area at the opposite end. "Miss Finch," he called out. "There be someone important here to see you."

She followed him back through the cave to

the service road. I could hardly stand to look at her in such a horrible condition. She gave me a blank stare, as if she didn't recognize me. Then, suddenly, she squinted at me like she was starting to remember. The instant she saw my star-shaped mole on the inside of my wrist she dropped to her knees before me.

I wanted to tell her that if perhaps she had shown just a little more love, a little more compassion for humans and animals alike, her life might have turned out much different, but I just couldn't bring myself to tell her that. I thought it might be too cruel, and besides, she couldn't turn back the hands of time to change the horrible thing that happened to her.

She slowly raised her chin and looked at me with tears beading down the sides of her cheeks. I was surprised to see real tears coming from her, for I never once believed in all my life that she was capable of shedding a single tear, even for herself.

I leaned forward and placed my hand softly on her shoulder. "Miss Finch, I want you to do one good deed in your life, and that is to show me where my parents are. I need you to take me to them. Can you do that for me?"

In a very weak and shallow voice she said, "But I don't know who your parents are."

Then I realized that she could never come to believe in the miracle that had changed me from the Mushroom Monster to my former self.

"Do you know where the Mushroom Monster parents are living now?" I asked.

She nodded.

"Would you be willing to take me to them?"

She raised both hands and covered her face in silence.

"I'm asking you a second time. Will you take me to the Mushroom Monster parents' house?"

She remained speechless.

"Oh, by the way, Miss Finch, did I mention that I just had a meeting with Mr. Brunsky, and bought your freedom."

She suddenly looked up at me. "The zoo owner?"

I nodded.

"You did that for me, after...?"

"The past is past. Mr. Brunsky couldn't resist the tidy sum of money I offered him to buy your freedom. I also told him that if anything like this should happen again, to anyone else, using deformed humans for public display, my husband, Prince Arnold, would deal with him personally. You're free to go. I only ask one favor in return for getting your freedom. I'm asking you one more time if you will take me to the Mushroom Monsters parents' house?"

She started to walk away, but then suddenly stopped and looked back over her shoulder. "OK, I'll take you."

Higgins fetched her black hooded coat to help keep her face hidden.

"I have just one special favor," she asked, "and that is never to let the Mushroom Monster's parents see me, or for you or Higgins to mention anything about me ever again.

I nodded. "Agreed."

The moment I stepped into the carriage, I heard Igor make three loud grunts. I turned and saw him staring back at us from inside his cage with his hand raised above his head, giving me the "V" for victory sign. I raised my hand and gave the victory sign back. I didn't think he knew what the sign actually stood for, other than something fun for the both of us to do together. However, I will never rule out the possibility that he really did believe the "V" sign stood for something good and positive.

CHAPTER 34

We traveled by carriage over hills and through valleys for several hours before we finally reached what I hoped to be my parents' house.

Miss Finch shouted out the window for Higgins to stop the carriage. Next, she pointed at a house perched on a high ridge, surrounded on three sides by tall pines.

"Is that it?" I asked. "Is that the Mushroom Monster's parents' house?"

Miss Finch slowly turned toward me, nodded, then took a shallow breath, and said, "Would it be too much to ask, before going there, to first drop me off at the nearest town?"

We already knew she didn't want to be seen

with her disfigured face, so we agreed.

After we dropped Miss Finch off at the nearby town of Everton, we bid her farewell.

A short time later Higgins stopped the carriage on top of the ridge beside the house. I saw a lady with white hair staring at us through the curtains. I wasn't sure if she was my mom or not, or if Higgins would even be able to recognize them for certain, since so many years had passed since his last visit.

We stepped down from the carriage and headed toward the house. The lady who I hoped to be my mom, Clarabelle, greeted us at the front door. "Can I help you?"she said with a smile.

That same moment, a man who I also hoped to be my dad, Devin, stepped next to her and placed his arm around her shoulder. I saw a picture hanging on the wall behind them of a woman about my age who looked like me. I believed the lady in the portrait was my mom when she was much younger.

I stepped closer. "Do you remember having a child long ago who was born with a disfigured face and body, looking like a monster?"

They glanced at each other in a moment of silence, then looked back at me and nodded.

"It is with great joy I wish to tell you that the

child born to you had a miraculous change, and is standing before you now."

They shook their heads with a look of disbelief.

Higgins spoke up. "Hear me. Remember, it is I, Higgins, the man who helped the zoo veterinarian deliver your baby. 'Twas a stormy night it was. 'Tis true, I witnessed the birth of your daughter, and am here again to give witness of a miracle come true. I be bringin' her back to you now, not as a monster, but as this beautiful young woman standin' before you."

My mom's white complexion started to show some color.

"Mom," I said, with tears starting to bead down my cheeks. "Look at the picture hanging on the wall behind you."

They both turned and looked back at the oil portrait, then back at me. My mom stepped closer and stared deep into my eyes. "Could it be? Could it possibly be true?"

Dad stepped closer and clasped my hand between his palms. "Could such a miracle happen to one, who once was such as before, who didn't even look human?"

I wiped the tears from my eyes. "An angel appeared to me one night with a message of hope, when it seemed no hope existed." I raised five fingers in front of them. "This is how many miracles I experienced in my life. The first one was that the face of horror departed from me. The second was being rescued from certain death by a giant whale. The third was finding my voice. And the fourth was becoming a princess in a faraway land."

My mom gave me a curious look. "Yes, but didn't you say that there be five miracles?"

I reached out and held my mom's hand. "Yes, of course, the last, and best of them all, is the miracle of being reunited with the both of you now."

Tears swelled in our eyes. I was so choked up with emotion I could barely speak another word. I tried to clear my throat. "I forgive you for whatever happened in the past. It is not to be mentioned again. I love you both dearly." I pointed toward the carriage. "Come with me. I want to bring you to a wondrous new land where I can cherish every moment of our future together."

We embraced and cried. Higgins pulled out his white cotton hankie from his breast pocket and blotted tears from his eyes.

I gripped Higgins's hand. "You have been like a guardian angel to me. Please say yes, and join us on a voyage to a new and wonderful land."

Higgins raised his hand to his chin, thought

for a moment, then spoke up. "But I would surely be a burden to you."

I smiled and shook my head. "To the contrary, you have been, and always will be a great blessing in my life. Did I mention too, that there are many guest rooms in the castle? One is waiting to be called your own."

The moment he heard that, his eyes stretched wide, and he gave me a big smile. "Well then, putting it that way... Let's be makin' a go of it."

Not long thereafter, my parents were packed and ready to go, and Higgins bother, Elroy, was hired to take his place as zoo caretaker. I felt confident that he would take good care of Zebu, Igor and the rest of the animals.

******

And so it came to pass, Mom, Dad, Higgins, and I boarded the clipper ship, The Bore Wind, and sailed back home to live goodly, happy, blessed lives, in the land of Nod, kingdom of Bore.

I made sure it wasn't boring anymore and arranged frequent musical contests and events. During any day of the year, one could see and hear people singing and practicing their musical instruments along the city streets, parks and outlying countryside. Music filled the air everywhere. It was truly now a land of pleasant melody, instead of a bore.

After we arrived back home, I shared with my parents all the details of my miraculous journey, beginning from the pits of my miserable past as the Mushroom Monster, to the final chapter of unspeakable joy, becoming a princess, and being reunited with them.

Higgins continued to make his paintings, and to my delight, his works came to be greatly admired and in demand at "The Gallant Knight" art studio in downtown Bore. It wasn't unusual to see art fanciers' line up before the store opened on Saturday mornings so that they could be the first to buy one of Higgins's new paintings.

But it was Higgins's nature to be happiest when he was helping others, so he quit doing paintings and instead started "The Higgins's School of Fine Art." From time to time, I would drop into one of his classes and watch his students receive instruction on how to add more strokes of color and beauty to a sometimes grey and dismal world.

Whenever my parents asked how I endured my past life as the Mushroom Monster, I loved to share with them the message I received from my guardian angel. "When your pain becomes so great you think you cannot bear it, you will have unspeakable joy, if you endure the trials, keep the faith, and live a life in love and kindness for others."

The final message I wish to leave with you now is that God loves you dearly. Embrace and follow the path of love, compassion, and forgiveness for a better and happier world for us all.

CPSIA information can be obtained
at www.ICGtesting.com
Printed in the USA
FSOW01n0835230116
15950FS